A FLICKER OF COURAGE

OF COURAGE

TALES OF TRIUMPH AND DISASTER!

DEB CALETTI

putnam

G. P. Putnam's Sons

G. P. PUTNAM'S SONS
An imprint of Penguin Random House LLC, New York

Copyright © 2020 by Deb Caletti
Map illustration copyright © 2020 by Adam Nickel.

G. P. Putnam's Sons is a registered trademark of Penguin Random House LLC.

Visit us online at penguinrandomhouse.com

Library of Congress Cataloging-in-Publication Data
Names: Caletti, Deb, author.
Title: A flicker of courage / Deb Caletti.
Description: New York: G. P. Putnam's Sons, [2020] | Series: Tales of triumph
and disaster! ; [1] | Summary: "Four ordinary kids must find the courage to
face their town's evil leader when he turns their friend into a naked lizard,
prompting an extraordinary adventure"—Provided by publisher.
Identifiers: LCCN 2019034034 (print) | LCCN 2019034035 (ebook) |
ISBN 9781984813053 (hardcover) | ISBN 9781984813060 (ebook)
Subjects: CYAC: Courage—Fiction. | Friendship—Fiction. |
Magic—Fiction. | Good and evil—Fiction. | Kings, queens, rulers, etc.—Fiction. |
Adventure and adventurers—Fiction.
Classification: LCC PZ7.C127437 Fl 2020 (print) |
LCC PZ7.C127437 (ebook) | DDC [Fic]—dc23
LC record available at https://lccn.loc.gov/2019034034
LC ebook record available at https://lccn.loc.gov/2019034035
Printed in the United States of America
ISBN 9781984813053

1 3 5 7 9 10 8 6 4 2

Design by Theresa Evangelista.
Text set in Cheltenham ITC Pro.

For John, Sam, and Nick, and for Erin, and Pat, and Myla—
timeless love to you, family.

And for Jen Klonsky and Michael Bourret—
with forever thanks and infinite exclamation points.

CHAPTER 1

The Backward Clock

On this Saturday morning, the Saturday morning that changes everything, Henry Every opens his bedroom window. Still wearing his striped pajamas, he leans far out. Even Henry knows you shouldn't do this, of course, but never mind that now. He sticks one ear toward the wind and listens as hard as he can.

There are a few things you need to know about Henry. He's a kind boy. He shudders when people are mean, and feels sorry for the losing team. He always says hello to dogs when he sees them sitting alone in cars, and when a cow is standing by herself in a field, he'll give a friendly wave. But he's also lonely. So lonely that he feels it like an actual ache in his heart. So lonely that he lifts his window like this every Saturday at sunrise, and every afternoon, and every evening, too. He lifts it even if the wind whips in or the rain drips down or the snow splats. In winter, when he sticks his head out, the end of his nose freezes, and on mornings like this, he breathes in the delicious smells of summer.

He doesn't lean out his window to take in the glories of nature, though. He leans out for a more important reason, a critical reason: to listen to the Dante family next door. And the best day to do this is Saturday, at a very early hour. If he sticks his head far out then, he can hear the Dante children watching an episode of their favorite show, *Rocket Galaxy*. If he sits just so and barely makes a move, he can hear laser swords clashing with laser swords and the *clink-zip* sound of shots fired from spaceships. He can hear Rex Xavier capturing the Rebels of Venus as a meteor smashes into a magnificent planet.

A Magnificent Planet

Henry loves getting to listen to his favorite television show. But what he loves even more are the other sounds coming from the Dante house. The family sounds. The giggles and teasing of the Dante children, and even the shouts of GET AWAY FROM ME! and LEAVE ME ALONE! and YOUR LEG IS TOUCHING MY LEG! In the evenings, he can hear the low murmurs of Mr. and Mrs. Dante discussing important but mysterious things like mortgages and carburetors and gallbladders. He can hear the rattle and clank of pans at dinnertime as the fabulous smell of a Meat Mayhem Loaf drifts over to his window.

A Meat Mayhem Loaf

And he can hear his classmate Apollo Dante just being Apollo Dante—practicing his spelling words with a confident voice, patiently explaining to his sister, Coco, how a radio works. He can hear the *thump, thump* of a baseball hitting the very center of Apollo Dante's mitt as he tosses it into the air again and again. Henry has lived next door to Apollo his whole life, and he and Apollo have been at the same school forever, but Henry can't even speak to him. Henry can barely speak to *anyone* at school, but with Apollo it's worse. Apollo is so smart and so astonishing that every, *every* time he asks Henry to play, Henry's voice glugs and splutters like a clogged-up toilet. All he can manage to do is shake his head to say *no* as his insides scream *yes*.

Honestly, every time *any* of the various members of the Dante family say, *Good morning, Henry!* or, *How are you,*

Henry? or, *Would you like to come over for dinner, Henry?* his cheeks flame hot and his chin tilts down and he feels an upsetting clash of joy and sadness in his stomach. This is hard to understand, let alone explain, but a very deep piece of Henry is sure that he should never have any of that lovely goodness that belongs to the Dantes, and that Apollo should never, ever even *see* the terrible horribleness that belongs to him.

So instead, he leans out his window and listens to them. And, wow, it's all wonderful. It's all reassuring and calm and happy. Since Henry's house feels empty, these smells and sounds fill him up same as Yummers With Cheese. Well, he's never actually eaten Yummers With Cheese. His parents would never let him have something that marvelous, not in a million years. But the point is, he loves what goes on at the Dante house. It makes him feel such longing that his chest hurts.

This morning, though, when he pops his head out, something is strange. Something is very, very strange. Eerie strange. It's quiet over there. Dead silent. There's not a tickle or a shriek or someone getting mad because they've just been pinched. No one is tattling or screeching from fun. No one is crying because their glitter ball just rolled into the garbage disposal. Rex Xavier's laser sword is not slashing and jabbing and ridding the earth of evil.

It's strange, and also worrisome. A bad feeling inches in. He stares hard at the Dante house. Henry needs glasses, but no one has noticed. So if you looked up at his window right then, you'd see a boy with thin shoulders and rumpled black hair, his eyes squinched in order to see better. From what he can tell, the Dante windows are shut tight on this warm summer morning. The cars sit still in the drive. Even the bright green blades of grass of the Dante lawn stand straight and unmoving.

It's weird, all right. It's making Henry quite nervous. Well, he has lots of reasons to be nervous anyway, but now he gets the shivery creeps, the kind where it seems like a mouse has just scampered up your spine.

And then he hears it. A horrible wail. It's the sound of a wounded animal or a heart breaking. A bunch of awful and shocking images flash across Henry's mind. His gut gives a wing-flap of panic.

He cranes his neck farther. This is extraordinarily inadvisable. Also terribly foolish. The whole top half of his body sticks out. One more inch, and he'll tumble forward like a rolled-up sleeping bag. His heart pounds. His striped pajamas get somewhat sweaty in the armpits. But this is when he finally sees Apollo Dante, standing right there on the sidewalk in front of Henry's house. That noise, that wailing—it's coming from Apollo.

Suddenly, Henry's doing stuff without even thinking about it. He backs up fast. Slams the window shut. He throws on a pair of shorts and a T-shirt. His knees look like a pair of tennis balls. The shirt is an old holey hand-me-down from his father. Henry's skin is so pale, you can practically see the highway of veins underneath. Still, you see something else, too. The tiny, flickery flame of a person who badly wants to have a friend. To *be* a friend. The golden hue of someone who might one day be a hero.

Here is another thing you need to know about Henry Every: Way down deep, in that quietest place where you keep secrets even from yourself, Henry holds a tiny hope. Maybe, just maybe, there's something else out there for him, something other than loneliness and hunger and hiding. He has felt this inside, a waiting, like a caterpillar wrapped up in its cocoon. He didn't know what to do with a feeling like that. So he tucked it far, far back in his mind, as if it were a present he might someday open.

And now, seeing Apollo in despair, the butterfly knocks at the cocoon, and the ribbon is flung off the gift. Apollo's tears send Henry down the stairs so fast, he's practically flying. He races past his parents and hurls open his front door. A different Henry steps outside, only he doesn't know it yet.

A story old and new begins.

But be warned, because in this story, there are slippery creatures, dark forests, and dazzling displays of courage. There is also evil, lots of evil, and a few near misses, and several daring escapes. It is a terrifying and nail-biting and nerve-racking tale.

One that unwinds, like a timeless, backward clock.

CHAPTER 2
A Terrible Spell

Henry has never seen Apollo like this. As you can imagine, he's seen Apollo in lots of situations—the day he crashed his skateboard and broke his wrist, the time he lost his Super Scuba diving watch, the sad occasion of the death of the classroom hamster, Polly.

Polly

Throughout those awful events, Apollo barely shed a tear. Now, though, his bike is sideways on the grass and he's

7

sobbing his eyes out. This, plus the shut-tight Dante house—it's all very alarming. Henry's stomach knots up. He's seriously scared. Something truly horrible must have happened, because, in addition to not being the crying type, Apollo does not have much to cry *about*. Not only is he smart, but he's handsome, too, and his new school clothes never seem to run out. If there's a coin toss, he wins it, and if teams are chosen, he's the captain. Now that it's summer, every boy and girl in the neighborhood has been at Apollo's big house, running through the sprinkler or squirting each other with the garden hose, screaming and laughing.

At Apollo's house, at least in the backyard and through the windows that Henry can peek into, there's every kind of large toy to jump on or ride in. There's every sort of ball to go into, over, under, or across every hoop, hole, or racket. At school, Apollo has snacks of every kind— crackers in the shape of animals, milk in rainbow colors. His face is quite frequently sticky with Jam Nougats and Cherry Freezees. In the winter, he wears a puffy jacket with five zippers and a secret inner pocket, which Henry saw when the coat was hanging on a hook at school. It was hard not to stare.

Even more astonishing than all of that—Apollo's parents kiss and hug him. They tousle his hair with pride. They wipe the splotch of Cherry Freezee off his face with a gentle thumb. Henry can barely believe that Apollo gets to live like this every single day. How incredible! At Henry's tiny falling-apart house next door, there's not even a basketball that goes *splat* when you try to bounce it, and he is never allowed to have snacks at all, even when his tummy is rolling with hunger. While Apollo gets sandwiches without crusts for lunch, Henry gets crusts without sandwiches. On the nights he gets to have a meal, it's the sad frozen dinner with the peas.

The Sad Frozen Dinner with the Peas

Sometimes, Henry envies Apollo, if he's being honest. And Henry always tries to be honest, as well as kind. These are the things that are his. He doesn't have jumpy castles and trampolines and Double Rocket Pops and parents who hug and kiss him, but he has kindness and honesty and a good heart. This doesn't seem like much quite a lot of the time. But Henry doesn't yet know that a good heart is the one thing every hero has.

Oh dear—the details are terrible, but facts are facts: Apollo's shirt is soaked with tears, and a river of snot flows from one nose hole. When someone who has everything in the world is bawling their eyes out, you know that things are bad.

"Rocco!" Apollo cries. "My Rocco! What am I going to do?"

Rocco? Henry's heart sinks. Rocco is Apollo's little brother. Well, his medium-little brother. His little-little brother is their new baby, Otto, and there's also Apollo's sister, Coco. Otto is bald and wiggly, and his arms are as plump as sausages, and he sometimes squalls like a fire alarm. But Rocco—he's one of those cute little kids with round cheeks, and he waits and waits at the window until Apollo gets home from school. Henry would be crushed if anything had happened to him.

And something else: As Apollo speaks to Henry on that sidewalk, Apollo is looking straight into Henry's eyes, *straight at him*, like you do with someone you know. Like you do with someone you *trust*.

The heat rises in Henry's face. His armpits begin to dampen. But now a small miracle occurs. Instead of his thoughts sticking in his windpipe like a hunk of bread, his voice rises up. It's a tiny bit quiet at first, but nonetheless there it is, speaking to Apollo in the bright shine of daylight.

"What happened? Is Rocco okay?"

Apollo holds out his arms. The morning sun wrongly beams down. Apollo's hands are cupped, and inside of the cup sits a lizard, an entirely unclothed lizard, no lizard trousers or lizard pajamas, or lizard anything else. A *naked* lizard.

Apollo—well, he seems to be indicating that Rocco is that

reptile. But that's ridiculous. It's hilarious. It's complete and utter nonsense. Rocco's a small boy with big curls and tennis shoes that light up and a backpack with a dinosaur on it. This is a naked lizard. Henry wants to laugh. In fact, he has to swallow down the burble of a chuckle rising up. He would never laugh, though. It would be cruel, because, well, look at Apollo. With all that crying, his eyes are like raisins in a muffin, soggy and shriveled.

Henry tries again. "Okay. You found a naked lizard. But what happened to Rocco?"

Apollo stares hard at Henry. And when he does, Henry's heart freezes and his breath stops in his lungs. Apollo's terror-filled look explains everything. This is Rocco, all right. Henry knows exactly who caused this torment.

Someone bad.

Someone so vile that he might cast a spell on you and turn you into your worst ugly nightmare forevermore.

Apollo can barely say the words. "Vlad," he chokes. "Luxor."

When Apollo says the name, Henry swears that the leaves stop shimmering in the trees, and the birds stop singing, and everything becomes so still that every slurp inside of every straw is silenced, and every wrapper has stopped crinkling mid-crinkle.

Henry shivers. "Oh no."

Henry wants to drop to his knees in despair. His whole body clutches up with anguish. Vlad Luxor is their Horrible Ruler with Magic. Vlad is so powerful and his temper is

11

so random that everyone in the Timeless Province is both terrified and at his mercy. His mood changes in an instant. It's impossible to tell what might happen next. There have been other HRMs in the eons of history, leading to long, yucky years of hideous hate and putrid power. But there have also been the majestic RMs, with no *H* at all, who made sure that you could rest easy, who brought peace and joy to the grown-ups and children and animals of the earth and the oceans far and wide.

Their last ruler was one of those. Best Farriver was good and decent, an RM through and through, though Henry's parents detested him. When Best Farriver sadly croaked of old age, they had no idea who would step up to fill his place. You never knew which particular child had grown up to discover that they possessed the *M*. Who had realized that they could make a dog fly instead of just sit, shake, or roll over? Who had begun to slowly see that they had the power to make people applaud or do good or do evil? It could be the best and brightest and kindest person or the worst, most insufferable one. Fate is unpredictable like that, Henry knows from personal experience.

To their great misfortune, after Best Farriver kicked the bucket, the person who came forward was Vlad Luxor, one of the H-est of HRMs in history. The first thing Vlad Luxor did was cover Best Farriver's beautiful old stone tower in shiny black mirrors. The next thing he did was put a high, frightening fence of iron bars around the entire base of

Rulers Mountain, which used to be open to everyone who wanted to shop in the small village at the top, or play in the grassy park in front of the tower. Now only Vlad's people were allowed in.

And then the real horror started. He turned the news anchor of WKZP into a zucchini just for speaking badly about him, and he transformed his own right-hand man, Devin Cowlick, into a crumbling statue for not admiring him greatly enough. He changed Ms. Bedlam's hair from brown to blond simply because he preferred it that way. A grandmother was zapped across the world, never to be seen again, for entirely mysterious reasons. He turned their science teacher, Mr. Neutroni, into a scary clown, because Vlad Luxor doesn't believe in science. This is shocking and almost too awful to believe, but some children were even put into cold, windowless rooms and *locked up*.

It's hard to truly know how much damage Vlad has done. How can you tell how many people have been turned into snakes or worse when snakes can barely speak above a whisper? When trees only shush? When clowns only honk annoying horns instead of using actual words? And the feeling of danger is everywhere, always. Henry feels it, like a ghost-shadow hovering over his shoulder. He gets the nervous creeps on every street in town. He carefully walks the halls at school, clutching his books to his chest. Whenever he goes through the town square, past the big billboard where Vlad Luxor's enormous image gazes down, he turns away as fast as he can, even on the good days when it is streaked with bird poop. Everyone whispers behind their hands that those birds aimed on purpose.

The thing is, there's Vlad Luxor's singular power and magic, and Vlad Luxor's one set of eyes and ears, but there are also Vlad Luxor's employees, like his new right-hand man, Mr. Needleman, whose job it is to know things even before Vlad Luxor knows them himself. There are Vlad Luxor's supporters, too, people who actually like him or are too afraid not to, people who actually can't wait to tattle about your possible wrongdoings so he'll maybe turn you into a badly carved jack-o'-lantern, with a single tooth held in place by a toothpick. You have to be careful. You can't tell who is who just by looking at a person. It feels like danger is everywhere, because danger *is* everywhere. Your neighbors might secretly work in Vlad Luxor's fifty-eight-story tower of black mirrors. A friend might turn out to be a spy. Even your own *parents* might praise his wise decisions and firm leadership.

"Are you *sure* that's Rocco?" Henry asks, hoping against hope that Apollo is wrong.

Apollo sniffs a long sniff of sorrow, and nods. "I'm sure. Show him, Rocco," Apollo says to the lizard.

Suddenly, a little pink bubble emerges from the lizard's mouth. It grows and grows until there is the tiniest, quietest *pop*.

"I taught him how to blow bubbles last week, and it's all he's been doing since."

All He's Been Doing Since

Henry leans down toward Apollo's hands. He smells the cotton-candy-like smell of Big Yum Bubble. The lizard makes a little squeak. And when he listens more closely, Henry hears actual words. He hears the lizard speak, and it is terrible.

"It's me, it's me, it's me," Rocco says, and waves his tiny arms.

CHAPTER 3
Rocco Disappears

Well, naturally, Henry is shocked to hear Rocco's voice coming from the naked lizard. And poor Apollo looks like he's been sent through a car wash without a car. Henry has no idea how to be a good friend here. And, wow, Henry would really, *really* like to be a good friend. The loneliness he feels at home is something he feels pretty much everywhere. He carries it like a loneliness backpack, from home to school and back again.

"This is horrible," Henry says.

"Rocco gets on my nerves, but he's still my little brother. I *love* him," Apollo says, sniffing. "And my mother has been crying her eyes out."

Oh, those words. Henry's insides bash around with feeling. He loves Apollo's mother. She's the nicest mother Henry has ever seen. She cuts sandwiches into triangles. She carries baby Otto on her hip, and claps with enthusiasm after Coco sings the *Rocket Galaxy* theme song while hopping on one foot at the same time. She helps out in their class at school, too, and when Olivia Pimento threw up in the hall one day, Mrs. Dante acted like it was one of the most natural things in the world, when it actually looked like a bad plate of Pasta Blobberini.

A Bad Plate of Pasta Blobberini

And Rocco! He has those little-kid knees that are always muddy and shoes that are always untied. He chases Apollo with the garden hose, yelling, *I'm a fidafighta!* when he means *firefighter.* This dreadful tragedy fills Henry with sorrow. And weirdly, because this is so unlike Henry, he's suddenly *mad,* too. When he thinks of a crying mother and a naughty brother who is loved regardless, he feels a rising hurricane inside.

"We've *got* to do something," Henry says.

"What can we do? It's hopeless."

Apollo has a point. It sure seems hopeless. The important grown-ups in the province they've always counted on before to save and protect are nowhere. The mayor has packed her bags and left. The police officers tremble and keep their mouths shut. The government officials have turned into spineless wimps. No one is doing *anything* to stop him. Vlad does whatever he wants.

And no one has ever been able to undo a spell, either. Well, this is not quite true—no one *today* can do the job. Over the years, there have been small groups of certain individuals—*spell breakers*—who could do it. Born with special abilities, of course, but also exceedingly brave, knowledgeable, and lionhearted, too, because undoing a spell is quite dangerous and no easy business. But not a single individual has stepped forward or even been identified. Worse, even *saying* the words *spell breaker* could bring great danger.

Why evil men have always existed, jumping out from the ickiest dark corners throughout our history—that is a true mystery, though. The minute Vlad arrived, their lives changed, *snap*, just like that. One day there were just regular problems like gross stuff under tabletops and people walking when the signs said Don't Walk, but now everything is a disaster. Vlad seems to hate whatever matters most. Parks with swing sets—poof, gone! Rocket ships—zap, vanished! Kind people who help old ladies—pow, you're out of here! Vlad strolls down the street of their town, pinching the bottoms of ladies like they are loaves of bread. He gazes at himself in store windows, smoothing his hair, which loops upward like a soft-serve ice cream cone. People tell him he's marvelous instead of disgusting. Slim instead of poochy. A great leader instead of a giant mess maker. It's a dark, dark time.

"Come on. I have an idea."

The words just pop out of Henry's mouth. He's surprising himself left and right. It's crazy, but all the things he desperately wants and all the things he so badly needs seem to be slamming together with the unfairness and wrongness he sees before him. An energy shoots through him right there on that sidewalk. His feet are moving toward his own front door.

His own front door.

This is a problem.

A big, big problem.

There's a particular something in there that might save the day, but his own house—well, it's not the best place to bring Apollo and Rocco. It's not the best place to bring *anyone*, which is why Henry has never done it before. There are dangers all around, and there's stuff Henry would rather keep secret. And there are dangers *specific* to naked lizards, too. Number one: Button, Henry's Jack Russell terrier. Number two: Henry's parents themselves. Number three: the Lewyt Deluxe, Model 55.

This is probably a good time to mention once more that Henry's home is not the haven of safety, security, and comfort Apollo's is. Imagine a world where fear and solitude meet. Where you're on edge every moment. Where there

No dust bag to empty!

LEWYT

WORLD'S MOST MODERN VACUUM CLEANER

The Lewyt Deluxe, Model 55

are bad moods, short tempers, and clouds of doom. One minute, you're smothered in a horrible hug, and the next, you are smacked repeatedly with the nearest object—a hairbrush, a cooking spoon. Henry's mother is large and angry, and she wears an old fuzzy bathrobe that smells of cooked cabbage. His father has mean, spiky hair shaved in a straight line across the back of his neck, and he stomps when he walks, and his bristles poke like slivers when he pretends to show affection to Henry in public.

Henry screws up his nerve, though, the way you do in an emergency. Apollo is suffering and Rocco is a lizard and Mrs. Dante is crying, so Henry leads Apollo across the scratchy brown grass of his lawn and up the two tilted steps to the door. He turns the handle warily. When he and Apollo step inside, Henry's father is doing his favorite thing: making a pyramid out of empty Pendleton Pale Ale cans. The television is blasting.

His mother is vacuuming, using the Lewyt Deluxe, Model 55. One of his father's socks disappears with a horrible screech, as if she's just sucked up a parrot, and the corner of the curtain is grabbed next. She wrestles it like it's a giant, thrashing serpent. Something smells like it's burning, and Henry guesses it is the beer can chicken that is his mother's favorite recipe.

It is going to be a long childhood.

"Henry?" Apollo looks at the scene before him with uncertainty.

"It's okay. Come on."

Well, it's not okay, not in the slightest, but for now, Henry, Apollo, and Rocco creep past Mr. and Mrs. Every and sneak up to Henry's room as Button

Beer Can Chicken

follows. Truthfully, sneaking isn't necessary. Henry's parents barely notice he's there unless he does something wrong. So he tries not to do anything wrong. His very own voice gets him into trouble, so he stays quiet as a moth in a closet. He does what he's told, and always uses his manners. When he talks back, it's only in his head, and even that makes him nervous. He keeps his room clean. In it, there's a small dresser and a creaky iron bed with a thin mattress. He also has a few secret prized possessions: his lucky marble, and two gifts from his grandfather—the book *Sinister Forces*, by Alvin Westwood, and a copy of *Amazing Stories* magazine, featuring tales of fighting evil.

Henry shuts his door without making a sound. Button lies on the bed with her chin on her paws, looking worried. Apollo paces.

"I don't know what to do," Apollo says.

"If we can find answers anywhere, it's here." Henry reaches under his mattress. His fingers wiggle until they grasp one of his *other* most prized possessions—an old, battered *Ranger Scout Handbook*, sixth edition, that he bought at their neighbor's yard sale for twenty-five cents.

Henry jumps immediately to the section on first aid. "How to stop severe bleeding. Artificial respiration. Something

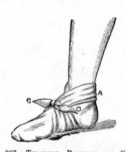

FIG. 367.—TRIANGLE BANDAGE ON FOOT. The foot should be placed on the triangle with the base *A* backward, and laid behind the ankle, the apex being carried upward over the dorsum or top of the foot. The basal ends *C* and *D* are brought forward, crossed, then carried around the foot, and tied on top.

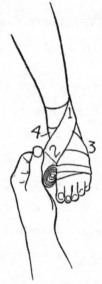

FIG. 366. — FIGURE-OF-EIGHT BANDAGE OF THE ANKLE AND FOOT. Numbers indicate route taken by bandage.

FIG. 368.—REEF KNOT.

How to Stop Severe Bleeding

in eye. Burns and scalds . . ." It's hopeless. There is nothing about turning naked lizards back into boys.

"Oh no!" Apollo suddenly says in alarm. "No!"

"What?"

"Where did he go?"

"What do you mean, where did he go?"

"He's gone! Rocco is gone! I put him in my pocket for safe-keeping, and now it's empty!"

"He can't be gone! This is awful! The world is a dangerous place for a lizard!"

"I know the world is a dangerous place for a lizard! There are birds of prey, and mammals, and lizards that eat other lizards, and parasites, and humans . . ."

Henry's heart sinks at the word *humans*. "Rocco!" he calls. "Rocco, where are you?"

Apollo is shaking out his shirt and—ugh—looking at the bottom of his shoes.

"Where would he go?" Henry asks.

"If I knew the answer to that, do you think I'd be in such a panic?" Apollo is on his knees, searching under the bed. "Rocco!" His voice is urgent and on the brink of despair. His eyes meet Button's from the bed.

"No. No, no, no!"

"Oh, Button." Henry feels sick.

"You didn't!" Apollo cries.

Button looks innocent. She's a good dog, a real friend,

but Henry forces her jaws open anyway, and peers into the ribbed cavern of Button's mouth.

"Nothing," Henry says. What a relief. If you're trying to become a best friend, you definitely *don't* want your dog to eat the person's brother.

"Thank heavens! But where could he be? He could be anywhere! He could be out in the street by now. He could be deep in a lawn, face-to-face with a mower! He could have run—"

There's a shriek from the living room below. A high-pitched, piercing SCREAM practically rattles the three coins in Henry's piggy bank, and causes Button to leap from the bed and bark in alarm.

Henry and Apollo look at each other with doom in their stomachs.

And then they hit those stairs in two seconds flat.

CHAPTER 4

A Devouring Beast

Rocco is clinging to a lampshade. Henry's mother wildly swings the gaping hose of the Lewyt Deluxe in Rocco's direction. This is terrible! What was Henry thinking? He should never, ever have brought anyone here. He's made the situation a million times worse. He's got to rescue that reptile and fast, but with all the shouting and clinging and the great, sucking hose, he has no idea how.

"Get over here, you little vermin!" Mrs. Every yells.

"Kill the ugly monster," Mr. Every says, bashing his bedroom slipper right and left.

Rocco's little tail is waving like a flag in the huge tornado of vacuum cleaner wind, and he is gripping as hard as he can with his tiny reptile toes. Poor Rocco is clearly petrified. He has lost his gum. Henry sees a tiny dot of pink right on the power button of his father's remote control.

"He probably jumped out of my pocket when he heard the vacuum!" Apollo says. "Lizards have very keen hearing, due to an absence of eardrums! They can hear better than snakes, even."

Henry admires Apollo's intelligence, but this is not the time for random reptile facts. "Get him!" Henry says.

Just as Apollo reaches out his hand, Rocco drops with terror onto the coffee table. He races like mad, right through the pyramid of Pendleton Pale Ale. The cans come tumbling down with a clatter. Mr. Every's face turns red, and his jaw gets tight, and Henry knows what this means: He's about to blow like a volcano.

When his father blows like a volcano, well, imagine a feeling where your insides curl up like one of those charcoal snakes you light on the Fourth of July. Where you wish you could drop through the floor and disappear forever. Where you're sure that hot lava will boil and burble over you until you become a fossil embedded in the earth.

A Fossil Embedded in the Earth

These are all the things Henry feels now. His shoulders hunch up in protection. The danger is a rumble underground, and there are tremors in the air itself. His father's eyes narrow into slits. His mouth opens until it looks huge and devouring. This is bad, but then things get worse. Rocco leaps from the table and lands on the back of Button, who jets through the living room and across the kitchen floor and out her dog door like she just robbed a bank and Rocco is the loot.

"ROAR," his father says. Or something like that. That's all Henry really hears.

"Run!" Henry cries, because the first order of business is escaping his father's meaty hand. They duck. Apollo flees from the room and races through the kitchen. Henry can practically feel the lava heat of his father's anger behind him.

Apollo flings open the back door. Henry sees Button, running at top speed. Button goes this fast only when she's dashing under the bed to hide from his parents, or chasing a squirrel, or when she's just grabbed the topmost prize, a chicken bone that missed the garbage can. Henry fears that an old chicken bone is not nearly as delicious to a dog as a fresh, wriggling reptile.

"Quick! Get her!" Henry shouts. They hurry out that door as Button's little white-and-brown backside rounds the corner of the house.

If you are also now worried that Button will take Rocco into her terrier paws, shove him into her mouth, and gnaw him to bits, imagine how Henry feels. Because right then, it seems fairly certain that Rocco will be lost forever in the twisty innards of Button's belly. This will be disastrous for Rocco, of course, but any dreams of friendship Henry has are also vanishing as fast as a rare bird in the wild.

A Rare Bird in the Wild

Instead of chewing on a delicious, satisfying lizard, though, Button is standing on the dry, scratchy front lawn, waiting next to Apollo's bike. Rocco is sitting upright on her back. This is surprising, but also somewhat of a miracle, given the general history of dogs and fast-moving creatures. Apollo puts his hand to his heart, relieved. Henry can't believe his eyes. He clutches his secondhand copy of the *Ranger Scout Handbook*, sixth edition, to his chest with joy.

"Button!" Henry leans down and scruffs her neck. He kisses her, big and noisy. Not right on the lips, but sort of. "Good dog!"

And then, Button does something else extraordinary. She paws at the bike. You know, like a dog in a movie. The champion dog. The best kind of dog that you want to fling your arms around and hug hard, even if there's no time for that.

"You're right. We need to get out of here," Henry tells her.

"This place is dangerous!" Apollo says. This is quite true. It's so true that for a second, Henry wants to cry the way you do when someone notices something you've felt for a long time.

Henry scrambles to the side yard near the garbage cans, where his old bike leans against the fence. It's a little rusty, for sure, but the bike is the last of his most cherished possessions. He bought it for two dollars at the neighbor's yard sale. He tucks his *Ranger Scout Handbook* under the nearby rhododendron for safekeeping.

"Follow me!" Henry says. This just pops out of his mouth, too. He has no idea where this sudden command has even come from. The little brother, the crying mother, the potential best friend, *evil*—it's made pieces in him whirl and shift and click into new places. On a normal day, he'd be huddled in his room doing homework, even though there was no homework, even though it was summer and school was out and everyone else was playing. Now, though, he just ran away from his father's roar, and astonishing stuff is bursting out of his mouth right and left. It's rather alarming. Even more: When he says *Follow me*, Apollo actually *follows him*.

Henry gets on his bike, and Apollo gets on his. The thing is, Henry knows just where to lead them. There's only one place to go when you need help this badly.

CHAPTER 5

Vlad Luxor Sends a Message

They pedal like crazy, their tires whirring and spinning. Button runs alongside. Rocco holds on, same as a cowboy on a wild horse.

"Hey, Henry!" Apollo shouts. "Where are we going?"

"The lighthouse!" Henry shouts back.

"The lighthouse? Are we even allowed to go there?"

"Trust me!" Henry calls.

And it seems as if Apollo does, because when Henry looks over his shoulder, there's Apollo, hunched down with speed, his tennis shoes a circling blur. Henry has made this trip many times, in secret, without his parents noticing he was gone, and so he knows the way. After their neighborhood ends, Henry will lead them into

*A Cowboy on
a Wild Horse*

town, down to the very end of Main Street. There, they'll take the dirt path through Huge Meadow. As the cobbled streets retreat behind them, they'll bend and weave through the glorious-smelling green and yellow grasses now packed with dandelions and wildflowers, until they reach the flat circular grass around the Y.

Now, though, Henry pedals through town, past the French bakery, the candy store, the Always Open Grocery. His tires bump along the cobblestones, past the brick buildings and lampposts. Today, there's no time to gaze at all the wonderful things in the windows that are never his—the glazed sweet rolls in the shapes of animals, the buttery braids of bread, the Rainbow Target Pops and Sugared Fruit Zips. His feet press hard on the pedals; his fingers grip the handlebars. He passes Big Meats, and Creamy Dreamy Dairy. Just as his front tire crosses into the town square at the very center of Main Street, though, he skids to a stop.

The big billboard with Vlad Luxor's image . . . Well, when he spots it, he's so shocked, and he brakes so fast, that his bike tires actually make an arc of black on the street. Behind him, Apollo screeches to a stop, too. Button freezes, staring upward.

"Oh man." Apollo's cheeks are red from pedaling so hard. His handsome forehead is sweaty. "Oh man, oh man, oh man, Henry. What is *that*?"

Henry has no idea, but it's alarming, for sure. As usual, Vlad Luxor smiles down from the enormous sign, wearing that black tuxedo with tails, a gold crown on his head. His chest is puffed out, his hair is perfect, and his teeth have the yellowish tint of an old pillowcase. But there's something new above the billboard. It's a long, thin screen with scrolling words, lit with blue lights. Maybe it's an ever-changing message or advertisement. Certainly, it's a new way of spreading misery. Along the street, men slide ladders and plunk equipment back into their trucks. There's the shuddering sound of doors slamming shut.

"I don't know, Apollo. It's like he's trying to talk to us."

The grocer from the Always Open steps outside and looks up, too. So does Ms. Esmé Silvooplay, the baker. A child and his mother come out of the candy store and look toward the screen, and so do people from the other side of the town square. Customers from the two fanciest restaurants, Rio Royale and La GreenWee, run out into the street with their white napkins still tucked into their shirts, toast still gripped in their fingertips, pancakes stuck on forks. Ms. Toomey, from Socket-Toomey Hardware, looks up and crosses her arms over her overalls. Henry spots Mr. Needleman, Vlad Luxor's new right-hand man, leaning against a lamppost, his arms folded in satisfaction.

Henry reads the words scrolling on and on. VLAD LUXOR MAKES YOUR LIFE BEAUTIFUL! VLAD LUXOR MAKES YOUR LIFE BEAUTIFUL! VLAD LUXOR MAKES YOUR LIFE BEAUTIFUL!

"It's a—" *Lie,* Apollo is about to say, but Henry claps his hand over Apollo's mouth. That mother with her child could be one of the people who leave baskets of fruit at Vlad Luxor's iron gate in that iron wall around Rulers Mountain. Even Ms. Silvooplay, unlikely as it seems, might be a spy who whispers things into Needleman's ear. The last thing Henry needs is *two* naked lizards on his hands.

Under the lamppost, Needleman whistles a cheerful tune. He adjusts his cuff links, entirely pleased with himself. He smiles as if he's done a good deed, and when he does, Henry gets that shuddery feeling you get when a person pretends to be one thing but is really another.

When a Person Pretends to Be
One Thing but Is Really Another

"Let's go," Henry says.

They get on their bikes and head off again. They ride through the town square, and all the way to the end of Main Street. They bump down onto the dirt road of Huge Meadow, but Henry's confidence has vanished, and his legs feel heavy. There's an enormous weight in his chest. Apollo is pedaling with great effort, too. When Henry sneaks a glance back at him, it looks like Apollo is about to cry. His shoulders slink. Even Button has slowed to a trot.

Huge Meadow feels especially huge. It's hard for Henry to remember that it's summer and that he's in a large and lovely expanse of yellow and green grasses with sweet-smelling flowers all around. The blades of passing weeds scrape his ankles, and dandelion fluff stuffs his nose, and by the time they reach the Y at the end of town, nothing feels very beautiful. In the spot of round, flat grass that surrounds the Y, Henry brakes to a stop. Apollo does the same. Button and Rocco stand still.

In the Circle of the Y, on a day like this, you can see the whole of Hollow Valley in front of you, and after that, the young green trees that mark the beginnings of the Wilds, the tangle of deep, thick forest that leads to the Jagged Mountains. When Henry squinches his eyes, he can actually make out their white, snowy tips marching unevenly across the blue of the sky. Button lifts her nose into the air and sniff-sniffs, and Henry is sure that she can smell the sun-warmed valley and the mossy darkness of the forest and the cold, sheer rock faces of the mountains. What's beyond the Jaggeds, though, no one knows. No dog could smell that far, either.

Even more important than the hinterland outstretched in front of them are the last two roads you can reach at this farthest-most edge of town—the one now on their right and the one now on their left. When Best Farriver was their ruler, either road was safe and fine, because everything all around was full of goodness. Today, if they take the road to the left, they'll wind down, down until they arrive at the beaming lighthouse at the edge of the Indigo Sea, but if they take the road to the right, they will come to a dead stop at the barred iron wall and the now-gated entrance to Rulers Mountain. Past that gate, the road winds up, up until it reaches the top, where Vlad Luxor's immense black-mirrored tower sits. The Wilds ahead, the Jagged Mountains, all that land between left and right—well, that's where things get murky. In all that middle ground, it's hard to tell exactly where you are, and if you venture into it, you could easily find yourself in places you hadn't intended.

Apollo gets off his bike. As he stands there with his feet planted in the Circle of the Y, he looks up toward Vlad's mirrored tower at the top of Rulers Mountain. It's so enormous that you can see it from anywhere in town, and from any distance. The tower rises to the sky, fifty-eight stories of black mirror stretching past the clouds. The mirrors reflect the whole sky and earth around it, but the images are dark and buckled and warped, and in those mirrors, the trees appear to stretch and tilt, and the sky slants. The shadow of the tower seems enormous, too. Enormous enough to maybe reach the sea, to cover the lighthouse, even.

"Do you think he can see us from here?" Apollo's voice is almost a whisper. This is not the same Apollo who slides into first base without even noticing the burn on his knees, or who stands at the map right in front of the class and points to Constantinople. Apollo looks as small and scared as a rabbit in the middle of the road.

Apollo and Henry and Button and Rocco—they *all* look very small with the mirrored building looming above them. You can feel a sudden and overwhelming helplessness when you are up against something so big and so bad. You can feel tears well up when a little brother has been turned into a lizard and is now riding on the back of a Jack Russell terrier. You can almost want to give up.

"I don't think he can see us. It's quite far," Henry says. His voice wobbles.

"The lighthouse seems very far, too," Apollo says. "I can't even smell the ocean from here."

The lighthouse. It's been Henry's only hope his whole life long. There, you can find practically all the wisdom in the world, and all the safety of a circling beam of light. But right then, every bad thing feels bigger than every good thing, which is almost the very definition of despair.

"It's closer than it seems."

Henry barely believes his own words. His voice is tired. His thin little legs are exhausted from all that pedaling.

"I don't know, Henry," Apollo says. "I mean, it's just you and me and Button. How can we turn Rocco back into a boy when we're not—" He doesn't dare say it right there in the open: *spell breakers*. But Henry understands anyway.

Henry looks up at the tower and its monstrous shadow, edging close. He feels what Apollo does, that they're a too-small army with no weapons. He wonders if goodness ever truly has a chance, which is a fair question, given Henry's life. And he realizes right then, too, that when it comes to goodness, you need all the people you can get.

"I just wish there were more of us," he says.

CHAPTER 6

Pirate Girl and Jo Join In

Picture words rising into the sweet, warm air of summer. Picture them lifting, like the fluff of dandelion seeds you make a wish on. Picture them being carried as if by magic to the exact place they need to land. This is what it feels like to Henry, anyway, because he has barely spoken the words *more of us* when something quite extraordinary happens. A lightning bolt of yellow appears in the center of the meadow road, and then a flash of red. His eyesight is bad, and so at first he can't be sure who is speeding toward them. But when they get closer, Henry's spirits do a cartwheel.

"Look who's coming!" Apollo shouts. "It's Jo and Pirate Girl!" Apollo's face has brightened, and suddenly he's like a dry plant that's been watered, and even Button starts hopping around on her hind legs as Rocco holds tight with all of his lizard toes.

And no wonder there's this sudden rush of joy, because aside from his grandfather, these two girls from his class—Josephine Idár and Pirate Girl—are the best, smartest, and bravest people Henry can think of. Once, Jo gathered two hundred signatures to remove the cruel principal Mrs. Gary, who used to pinch students on the soft part of their underarms. And when Mr. Morris Gene Glucose said girls were bad at math, Jo got everyone in their class to save their milk cartons for an entire month, since math is her favorite subject. They dropped the mountain of sticky, sour parcels on his desk, with Jo's note that read *23 × 30 = 690*.

And even though she's nearly as friendless as Henry, Pirate Girl is fearless. When a kickball whizzes over home plate, she sends it flying, and when a baseball zooms like a bullet right at her, she smacks it hard. Too, she fastened the horrid Arthur Farley to the flagpole using a rope and a clove hitch knot after he told her she was a stupid girl. She muscled Ginger Norton onto a cardboard sled and sent her sailing down an icy hill when Ginger called her ugly. And when Jason Scrum said she was weird, Pirate Girl put her fingers in her ears and recited all of the states and capitals and held her head high. Dealing with so many bullies has given her the kind of resolve and endurance only a few gain in an entire lifetime.

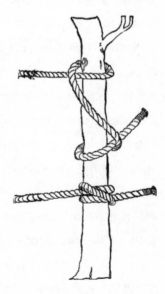

A Clove Hitch Knot

"Hey, guys!" Apollo calls, waving madly. Once again, Henry admires Apollo's self-assurance, because his own mouth gapes like a cave, and his stomach cinches up with nerves. If it took a great deal of guts to speak to Apollo, well, this will be a thousand times worse. Whenever Pirate Girl lunges in front of Henry to make sure he isn't struck by the ball in dodgeball, or whenever Jo offers him one half of her sandwich at lunch, not only do Henry's pits dampen as his voice sticks in his throat, but he also trembles inwardly, like a cupboard of dishes during an earthquake.

Jo's hair flies out behind her, same as the streamers on her handlebars, and Pirate Girl's face looks serious and determined. Strangely, it's almost as if they're heading straight toward them on purpose. The girls reach the Circle of the Y and stop.

"That's the fastest I've ever gone," Pirate Girl puffs, hopping off her bike. It's the most amazing bike you could imagine. It's a shiny red metal and has a bullet-shaped sidecar, which she built herself from a set of complicated plans. And Josephine Idár—*she* has a Schwinn Sting-Ray with all the accessories: banana seat, low rider handlebars, basket with flowers.

All the Accessories

"Me too," Jo says, hopping off hers. She takes a moment to ruffle the fur on Button's neck and look the dog in the eyes. Besides being kind to all human beings and animal beings, Jo is the most beautiful girl Henry has ever seen, with long dark hair and dark eyes. At school, her desk is as organized as the cockpit of a plane, and she once did a book report on all of the encyclopedias, volumes *A–Z*. It's her kindness, though, that really makes Henry weak in the knees. Now she reaches into the pocket of her denim shorts, which she wears with a T-shirt Henry has seen before—the one featuring Jo's long-ago relative and the subject of her oral report, Manuela Sáenz, revolutionary hero of South America.

"I can't believe you guys are here," Apollo says.

"We came because we both got one of these." Jo gives Henry a small rectangular sheet of paper. "A telegram."

"A telegram?" he manages to squeak.

"A message that's sent with electrical signals, which are then printed onto paper," Apollo says.

Manuela Sáenz, Revolutionary Hero of South America

"Mine's the same." Pirate Girl hands over a second sheet. Even though it's summer, she wears a leather pirate vest over her T-shirt, and mer, she wears a leather pirate vest over her T-shirt, and sturdy pirate boots. Like any good buccaneer, she's got a red pirate kerchief tied around her head, too, and colored beads woven into her brown hair.

Henry looks down at the paper, but the words blur from nerves. He tries to hold it steadily. He can hardly believe what the day has brought.

"We think it's from your grandfather, Henry. At least, it's signed *Captain Every*," Jo says.

"Captain Every is your *grandfather*?" Apollo's eyes go wide.

"You didn't know?" Jo asks.

"*I* knew." Pirate Girl hooks her thumbs in her pockets.

Henry feels a wind gust of pride. He can almost feel the sail of his personal ship fill in his chest.

"Well, they have the same last name, of course, but with Henry's parents, you'd never imagine they'd be relat—"

Pirate Girl glares at Apollo, and he stops midsentence. Henry's sail flattens, and the ship of his imagination vanishes just like that. People have noticed him more than he ever realized, which is both good and bad news.

"The telegrams were delivered right to our doors, and then we came as soon as we could. Pirate Girl caught up to me at the dirt path, and now here you two are. We have no idea why he asked *us* to come. Is it from him? Your grandfather?"

Henry stares down at the message. Parents and grandfathers and being noticed make the words jumble.

"Read it aloud," Apollo says.

Henry looks around cautiously. He's imagining . . . Well,

who knows what. A spider that can spy? A toad who can tattle? A pebble that can . . . Oh, whatever. You get the idea. With Vlad, any crazy thing is possible. But it seems like the coast is clear. Henry swallows. Takes a deep breath. *Three* people who might be friends . . . What a battle of nerves. The paper rattles, but he manages to read. "'A small Dante has been forever altered—STOP. Evil abounds—STOP. The time is finally right—STOP. To the lighthouse, pronto—STOP.'"

"He's talking about my brother Rocco, who's been turned into a reptile," Apollo says.

"Oh no! That's horrible! Poor Rocco! What do you think, Henry? Did your grandfather really send it?" Jo asks.

It *does* sound just like him. "I think so."

"Pirate Girl worried it was some sort of a trap. But maybe Captain Every thinks we can help," Jo says. "With all his wisdom and knowledge, he might have an idea what to do about this." Henry thinks the same thing, of course.

"I want to see the reptile with my own eyes," Pirate Girl says—rather threateningly, one might add. Being bullied has given Pirate Girl all of her best and worst traits.

Apollo plucks Rocco from the back of Button. Rocco dangles midair until Apollo places him in his cupped hands. The girls lean down and listen carefully.

"It's me, Rocco Dante," the lizard says. His voice sounds like a tiny, squeaky wheel.

"Holy cannoli," Pirate Girl says.

"This is heartbreaking. And the poor little thing is undressed besides," Jo says with her usual kindness.

"Well, if anyone would know what to do about Rocco, Captain Every would. I'm in," Pirate Girl says.

"Me too," Jo says.

Pirate Girl puts two fingers in her mouth and whistles. Wow! Henry's always wanted to know how to do that. Button's ears twitch. Pirate Girl points to her sidecar, and Button hops inside. Henry can see lots of stuff in there—rolled-up maps from various lands, a compass, a message in a bottle. She seems ready for anything.

"Let's get a move on, people," she says.

CHAPTER 7

An Entirely Different Tower

As they ride down the road to Henry's grandfather's house, Henry begins to smell the familiar smells of the sea: salt water and seaweed, plus the dead stuff that dogs like to roll in. Pirate Girl pedals hard, and Jo's hair flies behind her, and even Rocco, who's back in Apollo's pocket, seems to have forgotten his troubles for a moment. A truck passes, and Rocco pumps his tiny lizard fist, trying to get the driver to honk. The sky gets bigger as they get closer. Henry spots the twinkle of water, and then the white, glowing tip of Grandfather's house.

They drop their bikes outside the freshly painted fence of the keeper's quarters. The waves crash in and crickle out. The air is fresh and alive. Pirate Girl looks up toward the big lamp at the top of the lighthouse.

"Holy macaroni," she says. "Now, *that's* what I call a tower."

"I've never seen it this close before," Jo says.

"Me neither," Apollo says. "And look! From here, you can

see the set of highly polished prisms that create the lantern." Even Rocco's little beady eyes are wide.

This tower is very different from the black-mirrored building on Rulers Mountain. The lighthouse is a tall white column with red stripes, and Grandfather's majestic white house with red shutters sits alongside. It's bright and clean. You can see the beam of light for miles and miles. The lantern is lit in the day *and* in the night, in *every* kind of darkness and storm.

There's nothing better than a lighthouse with stripes, Henry's sure. He loves this place so much that his heart fills whenever he sees it. He loves everything about it. He loves the old tree out front, and the bank of ivy, and the white porch. He dearly loves what's inside. Henry wishes he could live here with his grandfather, but his parents would never allow it. They say that it's much too lonely a place for a boy. That it's dangerous. That his grandfather is a bad influence, even though everyone else thinks he's a great, wise man. To Henry, he's the greatest *everything*.

Pirate Girl runs up the porch steps and rings the bell before Henry can. Honestly, it's kind of maddening. But Henry hasn't eaten anything since last night, and he's ridden his bike a long distance in the summer heat, and he's dealt with quite a lot of intense emotion in just a few hours, so he might be a little testy.

The door opens.

And then there he is, in all his brilliance: Grandfather

Every, with his white beard and barrel chest, and his kindly eyes. He's wearing his blue captain's uniform, as always, pressed neatly, crisp as a just-made bed. He's beaming, same as that lighthouse. Henry smells biscuits baking. Suddenly, he's starving.

"Come in, come in, children! Welcome," Captain Every says. Henry hugs his grandfather hard around his waist, and his grandfather hugs him hard right back. Henry's head is held wonderfully against that big chest and that uniform, which smells like cold air and pancake syrup and salt water, or maybe those are just Henry's favorite smells. He feels a kiss on the top of his head. It's so wonderful, he wishes he could keep the kiss in a special box.

"Hello, Captain Every," Jo says, because she also has perfect manners. She shakes his hand.

"We got your telegram," Pirate Girl says, and shakes his hand, too.

Smart, valiant, and handsome Apollo has lost all words in front of the revered captain. His bottom lip begins to quiver. It's the kind of teary relief you feel when you finally hand over your troubles to a grown-up. He reaches into his pocket for Rocco. In his palm, Rocco jumps up and down and waves his arms. "We came for your help," Apollo says.

"Yes, yes," Grandfather says. "Your brother has been turned into a naked lizard by Vlad Luxor. Tragic."

"Why did you ask *us* to come, Captain Every?" Pirate Girl asks.

47

"I'm not sure what *we* can do," Jo says. "But of course I want to help if I can."

"Well, let's have something to eat first," Grandfather says. "And then we will discuss the matter."

In the dining room, there are warm biscuits with jam and butter, slices of Ham Haven, a Chilled Cheese Mondieu, and an impressively tall Jell-O mold. There's a bowl of water for Button beside a plate of Canine Crunch. There's a cricket on a lettuce leaf for Rocco.

An Impressively Tall Jell-O Mold

It's such a large and incredible feast, it must have taken hours and hours to prepare. Grandfather must have begun stirring hot water into gelatin even before Rocco's spell, Henry realizes. His grandfather is admired for his wisdom, of course, but how would he know something before it even happened? This is no time for quiet thoughts that you keep to yourself, though. "It's almost like you were expecting us," Henry says.

"Well, I have been," Grandfather says. "In fact, I've been waiting for this moment for a long, long time."

CHAPTER 8

The Awful Scene in the Always Open

Oh, the food is delicious. The biscuits are buttery and flaky, the ham is salty, and the cheese is creamy. The Jell-O is cold and wiggly, and slips down the throat like a raft on a waterslide. Even Apollo has momentarily put aside his troubles and is licking his fingers.

Henry is stuffed. Jo wipes her mouth with her napkin. Pirate Girl lets out a deep, satisfied sigh.

"Are we finished? Nothing like a good meal to get the gears turning." Captain Every taps his temple with his finger. "Shall we move to the living room?"

It's one of Henry's favorite rooms in the house, but not *the* favorite. He has seen this room many times before, when he's snuck out of his own dismal house to come here, but his friends haven't. So, Pirate Girl races to one wall and examines the painting of schooners on the high seas. Jo settles into a big cozy armchair next to a lovely statue of a mermaid. Apollo carefully spins the wooden captain's wheel set on a

The Painting of Schooners on the High Seas

brass stand in the corner. Button curls up on the braided rug in front of the fireplace, while Rocco finds the circle of sun made by the telescope, which points out the window toward the ocean.

But then, Grandfather clears his throat. There are urgent matters to address. Pirate Girl finds her seat—the wooden swivel chair embossed with an anchor. On the old leather couch, Henry sits on one side of his grandfather, and Apollo sits on the other.

"Now," Grandfather says to Apollo, "if we are going to right this terrible wrong, we need all the facts. Begin at the beginning. It is impossible to begin at the end, and the middle will remain a muddle if we don't start at the start."

"All right," Apollo says. "Well, very early this morning, we went to the Always Open Grocery because we ran out of milk." His eyes begin to water at the memory. "We're always running out of milk."

"Hmm, yes. One does," Grandfather says.

"Otto was in the cart, and our mother was pushing it, and Rocco and I were next to her. Rocco kept asking for things. 'Can I have Twisty Nibblers? Can I have Fried Crunchies? I want Lemon Zippers.'"

"Ugh," Jo says. "I hate when my little sister does that."

"He was popping his gum. He was blowing big bubbles that splatted across his whole face and had to be pulled from his hair. He's been like this all the time lately, since Otto was born. Annoying. Following me around. Poking my tummy when I'm trying to read *Great Moments in History*. Begging Dad to have staring contests when he's getting ready to go to work. Showing Mom how long he can hop on one foot while she's on the phone. Coming in my room and touching my stuff, and then singing *I'm touch-ing your stu-uff*. Putting his face into Otto's face and burping. Crying real loud when he isn't even really hurt. I could give a million examples."

"Frustrating, indeed," Grandfather says.

"And then, at the Always Open, he began to shout, 'I want Egg Jells! Give me Egg Jells!'"

"Gross." Pirate Girl makes a face.

"Disgusting," Jo agrees.

"No one likes Egg Jells," Henry says.

"Exactly! He was asking for things he didn't even want. 'You don't even like Egg Jells,' I said. And then Rocco started to copy me. 'You don't even like Egg Jells,' he said back."

Everyone looks at Rocco, who now snoozes in the circle of sun, because it's way, way past his naptime.

Apollo continues. "'Stop it,' I told him. "'Stop it,' Rocco said. 'I mean it.' 'I mean it,' Rocco said. 'Mom!' I shouted. 'Mom!' Rocco copied."

"Grrr. That's so maddening," Jo says.

"And here's where things really go wrong," Apollo says. "Mom turns to Rocco and says, 'You better quit that right now or you'll be sorry.' And then Rocco says . . ."

They all wait.

"*'You better quit that right now or you'll be sorry.'*"

Henry gasps.

"My mother's face turned the color of an eggplant."

"Purple?" Pirate Girl says.

"Red is mad. Purple is *furious*," Apollo says.

Henry can't even imagine Mrs. Dante getting angry, though he supposes all mothers have their

An Eggplant

limits, probably quite often reached in the grocery store.

"'Rocco Xavier Dante . . . ,' my mother warned."

They all hold their breath. Henry is hoping, hoping, hoping Rocco won't do what he fears he'll do.

"'Rocco Xavier Dante . . . ,' Rocco copied."

"Oh no," Jo says.

"Oh *no!*" Henry echoes. He shudders, imagining what would have happened if that had been him.

"My mother reached for his collar, but Rocco darted away. He darted as fast as a . . . well, a *lizard*. My mother tried to catch him. She steered the cart all over the place. It was the one cart with the squeaky wheel, and it kept making an awful *screech screech* whenever she went around a corner.

"Otto started to cry. Everyone was staring. And then Rocco zipped around a bend and crashed into a large display of Power Zaps. They came tumbling down, making this huge racket. I squinched my eyes shut. It was all too hard to watch."

Henry wants to squinch his own eyes right now.

"And when I opened them, I saw something horrible. Rocco was gone. And in his place was a naked lizard sitting among the Power Zaps."

"This is horrible," Pirate Girl says. She is twisting one of the beads in a lock of her hair.

"My mother screamed. Every single person was looking at us, but they'd stopped talking or even moving. You could see the fear on their faces. Vlad Luxor himself must have been there, in the frozen food aisle, or maybe in fruits and vegetables. It was the worst moment of my life."

Apollo sits back, exhausted. Jo is speechless, and Pirate Girl lets out a gloomy whistle of *wow*. Henry's stomach aches with sadness.

"I see," Grandfather says. "Your brother has been trying to get attention. In the Always Open, he was getting plenty of it. And Vlad Luxor hates when other people get attention. *Hates.*"

"Why a lizard, though?" Pirate Girl asks. "Why not a scurrying mouse, or better yet, a silent statue?"

"*Why?* This is the first thing you need to know, my friends. There is never *logic* in evil acts. Evil is power run amok. This way, that way, upside down! There's no point in searching for reason in the unreasonable! A madman does what a madman wants to do. Random, inexplicable acts cause the greatest uncertainty and fear. Irrational fury smushes your spirit like brown spots on a banana. *Why* is a waste of precious minutes. The only real question is *What are we going to do about it now?*"

Grandfather is slightly flushed from his speech. He shakes his head as if there are too many things he'll never understand, and then he folds his hands and sighs. For a long moment, he stares outside, toward the wide blue sky and the endless sea, as if he's imagining the past and the present, both.

They hear the tick and the tock of the clock on the mantel. The waves come in and the waves go out. No other great, wise words come pouring forth from Grandfather's mouth. They wait for an ingenious plan, but he's silent. He strokes his beard and they lean forward in expectation, but . . . Nothing.

Apollo clears his throat, as if he's nervous to interrupt the thoughts of the important captain. When Apollo finally speaks, his voice is a hesitant whisper. Of course, it's not just bad manners he's worried about, even though it's clear that there are no spies at Grandfather's house. "Um, Captain Every?"

"Yes, son?"

"Is there anything we can even do without a . . . *spell breaker?*"

"Of course there is nothing you can do without a spell breaker!" Grandfather says.

In an instant, Apollo's eyes turn to two shining pools of tears. Jo puts her head in her hands.

"I don't know why we're even here," Pirate Girl says.

"There's no hope, then," Apollo says.

Henry feels the very familiar sink of terrible-awful that means this is entirely his fault. They rode all the way out to the lighthouse to help Rocco, but it was pointless. His grandfather called them together with a telegram, and it was a total waste of time. In moments like these, other children might understand that this was not their fault and that they had tried their best. But Henry never feels that way. Instead, a tunnel of sorrow and a weighty guilt goes straight through him.

And what's even worse: He has let down the three people and a lizard who could have been his friends.

CHAPTER 9

A Most Magical Place

That horrible feeling—well, thankfully it lasts only a moment.

"No hope?" Grandfather says. "Don't be ridiculous! This is the most hopeful day we've had in years!" He rises. He heads toward the strange contraption near the fireplace. It's a large, round brass dial on a stand, with words like *Full*, *Half*, *Slow*, and *Dead Slow* written in a circle. Henry knows what this contraption *does*, but before today, he has never known what exactly it *is*.

"An engine order telegraph!" Apollo wipes his eyes and jumps up to look. "I read about these in *The Sinking of the* Titanic *and Great Sea Disasters*."

Apollo bends over the machine. His eyes light with curi-

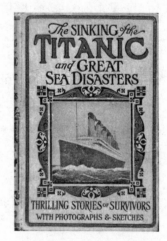

The Sinking of the *Titanic* and Great Sea Disasters

osity, and his cheekbones are high, and he still looks hand-some, even after all they've been through. Jo seems to notice. She gazes at Apollo with admiration. It makes Henry feel the slightest twinge of disappointment.

"What does it do?" Pirate Girl asks. "It looks amazing."

"On a ship, this is how the captain in the bridge talks with the officer in the engine control room," Apollo explains.

"Let's just say it communicates a change in direction." Grandfather turns the dial from *Stop* to *Full Ahead*.

At the turn of that dial, any disappointment or guilt or bad feeling Henry had vanishes. Now he's filled with a surge of excitement. "Come on, you guys!" he says, and heads for the door. Button rises to her feet, too, and jumps up around Grandfather's knees. Henry and Button know something that even Apollo doesn't: Apollo and Jo and Pirate Girl are about to see the most astonishing, and the most amazing, and the most *hopeful* place you can imagine.

Apollo tucks a drowsy Rocco into his pocket. They head down the path that connects the living quarters to the lighthouse. Henry's insides are leaping with glee, the kind of glee you feel when only you know the wonderful secret that's about to be revealed.

Pirate Girl skips ahead. "I love it here," she sings to the sky.

Well, who wouldn't? The lighthouse is the kind of place you just have to explore. When you're there, you want to race around its bottom, and climb to its top. You want to hide while someone seeks. You want to run while someone chases and chase while someone runs.

Captain Every's command on the engine order telegraph has reached his officer in the engine room. Or rather, Grandfather's message has reached The Beautiful Librarian, who now stands at the open door of the lighthouse. The Beautiful Librarian has an elaborate hairdo, sprayed to perfection, and a pair of serious glasses perched on her exquisite nose. She is always ready to shush, or turn a page, or pluck a volume from a shelf.

Elaborate Hairdo, Sprayed to Perfection

More than that, though, whenever Henry visits, she is always ready to gather him in a hug, or show him an unusual beetle, or hand him a tissue just when he needs one. When he stumbles, The Beautiful Librarian never points and laughs like his father does. Instead, she bends down to check his knees for scrapes, and asks if he's all right.

"Henry," The Beautiful Librarian says. Her eyes light up when she sees him, as if his presence actually makes her happy. To Henry, this seems incredible. There's the fragrance of lotus blossoms as she leans down and kisses his cheek, too. His heart fills, and it's another kiss he wishes he could keep forever. "Button," she says, and pats the dog's delighted head. "And you must be Apollo. And Jo. And Pirate Girl." Henry can't imagine how she knows his classmates, who now wait at the entrance to the lighthouse. Of course, librarians know many unexpected things.

"Well, Big," she says to Captain Every, "the children have arrived."

"Yes, darling," he says. "Lead the way."

The children have gone nearly speechless at her beauty. They move forward in a thunderstruck huddle. Then Pirate Girl lets out a squeal, because she can't wait to see what's beyond the door.

And what's beyond the door? Well, at first you see only the small and tidy living quarters of The Beautiful Librarian. While Grandfather's house is huge and sprawling, with ceilings so tall, they're the perfect haven for a spider or two, The Beautiful Librarian lives in a small square room that's snug and comfortable and shipshape. It has everything a person might need—charming windows with many panes that look out toward the sea, an inviting reading chair, and a roomy down bed with the fluffiest of pillows. There's a kettle and a small stove, and there are tins of butter cookies.

But something else soon catches your eye.

Something immense.

Something magical.

Something that you've never before seen in your life.

A spiral stairway. A stairway that curves up toward the very top of the lighthouse, where the huge lantern spins its beam.

But this is not just any spiral stairway. It's colossal enough to take your breath away. And its walls . . . Well, they're covered in books. Books, and books, and more books! The lighthouse is the most astonishing and astonishingly tall library you could ever imagine, with book after lovely book rising toward the sky. There are shelves and shelves of ancient books, all with that fine and musty old-book smell. There are shelves and shelves of dazzlingly shiny ones, each with that delicious new-book smell. There are red books and blue ones, fancy books and plain ones. Books tiny enough to fit on your thumb. Books large enough that they couldn't fit back out the door.

When you first see it, you want to dash up the stairs, dragging your fingers along every spine. You want to stand at the bottom and look up, and stand at the top and look down, so that you can take in the enormous number of books and books and books. You want to grab greedily, fling and open, feast your hungry eyes on all those words and words and pictures and pictures and adventures and voyages and knowledge. You want to smooch the spines and bite into the pages. You want to chew the sentences and swallow up the paragraphs.

But you also want to stand in hushed respect, too, and that is what they all do first. Button sits like a good dog, chin high, gazing upward. Rocco is fully awake now, and even he is respectfully silent. They blink and blink at the enormity of that enchantment. The only thing they can do is take in the moment, the moment where they understand for the first time that beyond one door there can be thousands of others.

CHAPTER 10

The Impossible Solution

O f course, a terrible thing has just occurred. A brother has been turned into a naked lizard. The day has brought unforeseen stress and trauma. There is still no solution in sight. Clearly, there are more difficult and challenging events yet to come.

Still, even in the direst circumstances, one must take in beauty and magic when it's right there in front of you. So, before getting down to business, the children stare from the bottom up, and race to the top to look down—at the books, at the sea stretching out, at the enormous lantern with its many-sided glass. Apollo tips the book spines and smells their pages. Rocco tries to annoy his brother by covering random words with his bottom and wiggling it so that Apollo can't read. Pirate Girl gazes at a few glorious and extravagant images of lions and jungles, sea monsters and foreign lands. Jo hugs a red velvet volume to her chest. Henry and Button look with wonder at the greatest hope they have against evil: knowledge and light.

Extravagant Image of a Lion

Finally, the *keeper* of the knowledge and the *keeper* of the light look at each other and nod. "It's time," The Beautiful Librarian says to Captain Every.

"Come, children! Spells!" Grandfather calls in a big, booming voice.

The word *spells*—it's like a command, an invitation the children can't help but answer. They run from their various spots in the library to gather around a curved table in the middle of the lighthouse, where The Beautiful Librarian has already stacked the thick, dusty tomes. They're dusty enough to make Jo sneeze. Henry's heart beats with excitement when he sees one particularly enormous book. He's dying to touch it. The cover is leathery, and the edges of the pages are a dim gold. When Captain Every opens it, Henry sneaks his finger out to feel the ancient, crispy paper.

"Excuse me, Captain Every," Apollo says. "Can any of these books even help us without a . . . you know."

Grandfather ignores the question. "Lizard, lizard . . . ," he says. He and The Beautiful Librarian are both scanning the index of the giant book.

"Wait," she says. "What am I thinking? There are—"

"Five thousand six hundred species of lizard on earth!" Apollo says.

"Exactly." The Beautiful Librarian smiles. "Let's try this another way. Spell characteristics?"

"Reptilian," Captain Every says. "Butt naked."

Pirate Girl giggles. So does Henry.

"Big. *Please*. Without clothing," she corrects. "Preexisting conditions of the victim?"

"Brattiness, show-offiness, begging for attention."

"Ugh," The Beautiful Librarian says.

"Copying in an annoying fashion," Grandfather says.

"Copying in an annoying fashion," The Beautiful Librarian repeats with a wink.

"You better quit that now or you'll be sorry." Grandpa winks back.

"Here," The Beautiful Librarian says, pointing. Henry stands right beside his grandfather and looks down. Pirate Girl stands at his other side. Rocco is sitting on the desk, looking quite small compared with the giant image of the lizard in the book. Apollo and Jo are on the other side of the table, way too close together, in Henry's opinion.

"*Lizardo Nakedismo*,'" Grandfather reads. "Yes. This must be it. Oh, how awful. 'Duration, permanent.'"

Apollo looks like he might cry again. Jo notices, too, and takes Apollo's hand, which is rather yucky for Henry to watch. Rocco looks distraught. If you've never seen a distraught naked lizard, be advised, it is an extraordinarily upsetting sight.

"Is it all coming back to you, Big?" The Beautiful Librarian asks Grandfather.

"Ah, it most certainly is," he says.

"What's this part?" Pirate Girl asks. She's reading ahead. Reading ahead can always get on your nerves, though maybe Henry's mood was already turning a little sour. Gushy handholding can sometimes do that to a person.

"This is where *you* come in," Grandfather says, and then he fixes each and every one of them with a serious gaze. "It's the section for the spell breakers."

"The *spell breakers*?" Jo asks. She drops Apollo's hand.

"Mmm-hmm." Grandfather silently reads.

"I thought we didn't have those anymore."

Henry has no idea what his grandfather is saying. The words alone make him kind of nervous, to be honest. Maybe a little more than nervous. Actually, he feels pinpricks of dread trickle up his arms. Apollo seems uneasy, too. He runs his hand across his forehead, and Jo begins to bite the nail of her thumb. Button lies low on the floor, chin on her paws, one ear twitching. Only Pirate Girl leans forward eagerly.

"There are *always* spell breakers," Grandfather says. "In every generation throughout history. Sometimes, they're just not needed. Now, however, you are very, very badly needed."

"You're not really saying that *we*—" Pirate Girl's eyes go wide.

"Oh yes. Why else do you think I've brought you all here?" Grandfather says, still perusing the book.

"To give us your great wisdom about Rocco's situation?" Apollo's voice has turned quite high.

"This is the greatest wisdom I have." Grandfather's eyes move across the page.

"I've never broken anything before," Henry says quietly. "Let alone a spell."

"I once broke my humerus," Pirate Girl says. "Which was actually quite serious."

"I once broke my mother's favorite garden-gnome music box," Apollo says. "But I bought her another one with my birth-day money."

"This is an entirely different kind of breaking. And it must be done only by an entirely dif-ferent type of person. Or *per-sons*." Now Grandfather looks up, and he does it again. That

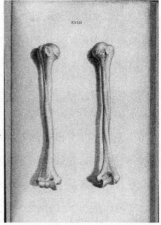

A Serious Humerus

nerve-racking thing where he looks hard at each of them in turn.

"Us?" Henry asks.

"You," Grandfather says.

Garden-Gnome Music Box

"I'm pretty sure I'm just a regular girl," Jo says.

"Holy ravioli! We're spell breakers? This is fantastic!" Pirate Girl shouts. "Look at my arms! I have goose bumps."

"Isn't spell breaking extremely dangerous?" Drops of sweat gather on Apollo's forehead.

"Well, of course it is! But this poor child has been turned into a naked lizard. A brother. A son!" Grandfather holds his hand out to indicate Rocco, who is utterly silent, not a noise coming from his tiny lips. "And *you* can make it right. What a glorious opportunity! What a fine responsibility, to do good in the face of evil! We have an HRM running around like a maniac."

Henry's head begins to throb. He wants to help Rocco, but the idea that he himself might have to break a spell, or *many* spells—well, it's a great deal more than he bargained for. He's heard only a few whispers about the spell breaking of the past, but they were rather alarming whispers—*Danger. Peril. Spine-chilling, knee-knocking, wet-your-pants fear.*

"'*Lizardo Nakedismo*, spell-breaking option one. Take a sailing vessel to a distant country . . .' Well, that won't exactly work this time, will it, my dearest?" Grandfather says to The Beautiful Librarian.

"Not this time. Read on."

"'Option two. Gather a lantern, two black shoes, a compass, one very large piece of toast, a can of sardines, a foldout map of Australia . . .'"

"Wait," Pirate Girl says. "What did you say? Hold on! Stay right here! I'll be right back."

She takes off. Grandfather removes his pocket watch from his jacket and keeps his eyes fixed on the second hand. Henry hears Pirate Girl's feet, running down the lighthouse stairs. The door opens, closes, and opens again. Up the stairs she comes. She's out of breath, and her face is flushed. She drops a pile of gear on the floor, startling Button to her feet.

Grandfather looks at his watch. "Sixty-two seconds. Extraordinary."

"A lantern," Pirate Girl puffs, out of breath. "A compass. A can of sardines. A foldout map of Australia . . . All we need are the two black shoes and a very large piece of toast."

"Wow," Henry says. He knew she had a lot of stuff in that sidecar, but he's quite impressed.

"Maybe helping Rocco will be easier than we thought," Jo says nervously. "Maybe it'll be all right. I eat toast almost every morning."

"This is an excellent beginning," Grandfather says to Pirate Girl. He beams at her, and she beams back. "However, one must always remember to turn the page."

Which is what he does next. "'Eyelash from a white rhino,'" Pirate Girl reads.

"One of the rarest creatures in the world." Apollo sighs. "Next to the northern hairy-nosed wombat and the pygmy three-toed sloth."

"One must always remember to turn the page, but one must always remember to read the fine print, too," The Beautiful Librarian says.

Henry squinches his eyes. He can barely see the tiny words written below *option two*. They are the most minia- ture black swoops and swirls, as though a tiny ant forgot to wipe his feet before he tromped across the page.

The Beautiful Librarian slides her glasses down her nose and reads, "'In the dreadful and appalling circumstance that option one and option two are not options, there is the optional option three. This is the Hiding in Plain Sight cure. Victim must be paraded in full view of the spell caster with- out being seen. Of course, this is impossible and dangerous and therefore utterly inadvisable.'"

Apollo looks sick with fright. And Rocco himself has gone from a deep green to a light olive. "Does that mean what I think it means?" Apollo asks, horrified.

"Are you saying we have to take Rocco somewhere where Vlad Luxor can see him, only he can't be spotted?" Jo's beautiful brown eyes are dark caves of terror. For a moment, they are all so silent that Henry can hear the sea crashing against the rocks.

"Yes," Grandfather says, nodding. "And yes again."

"But Rocco can't be trusted not to try to get attention at

the worst moments," Apollo says. "Even when you try and try to tell him to behave."

"And this means that *we* will also be visible to Vlad Luxor," Pirate Girl reminds them.

"Precisely why it is impossible *and* dangerous," Grandfather says.

"I don't know," Apollo says. "I mean, we could . . . adjust. To having a reptile in the family. I could maybe make Rocco a bed out of a box of matches . . ."

Now, along with his pounding head, Henry's tummy tumbles with anxiety. He can't understand how they've gone from being regular children to spell breakers in an afternoon. The words *peril* and *spine-chilling* and *knee-knocking* echo in his whole body.

But then it's there again, the same feeling he had that very morning—a flickery flame in his chest, that golden-rise of something he can't name. Henry thinks of the broken-hearted Mrs. Dante, and the times he's seen little Rocco riding his trike as fast as he can. He thinks of the times he's heard the Dante family laughing through his open window at night while he lies in bed. That laughter seems like the most beautiful sound in the world. It's a sound worth fighting for.

"I'll go alone, if I have to," Henry says.

"You don't have to," Pirate Girl says. "I'm going, too."

"All right," Jo says with a solemn nod. "Same for me."

"I guess I will," Apollo says, somewhat reluctantly.

Rocco has had enough of being still and quiet. He's climbed to the top of Apollo's head and now droops his tail over one of Apollo's eyes. He is snapping his fingers and hopping from foot to foot, doing a silly dance in case anyone has forgotten about him.

"La la la," he says in his tiny naked lizard voice. "Pee pee pee."

They're doomed.

CHAPTER 11

The News That Comes with the Pink Mebiolo

In Grandfather's dining room, he reaches into a large cupboard and removes several small glasses. They are made of blue and green sea glass, same as the floats from old ships. The children sit once again at the heavy table as he rummages in a drawer and finds a tiny thimble as a cup for Rocco, who's perched on the curved cover of the butter dish.

"I think this calls for a celebration," Grandfather says. "Would you mind, darling, fetching that bottle of sparkling Pink Mebiolo from Mrs. Walden Thackaray?"

"Oh, Big, you've forgotten. I don't fetch."

"Quite right. My bad. I'll be back in an instant. Can you remind me which one it is again?"

"The dusty bottle in the center of the bottles," The Beautiful Librarian says.

Grandfather dashes away and returns in seconds.

"This one, my dear?"

"That's it."

Grandfather Every hands the bottle to The Beautiful Librarian, and she releases the cork with a loud *pop*. The sound causes Button to bark like someone's coming, same as she does whenever a doorbell rings on TV. The liquid is a slightly dirty pink, like a smoggy sunset, and maybe there were bubbles once. Pirate Girl sniffs her glass, and decides to sip.

"I don't understand. How is it that we could be normal children one minute and spell breakers the next?" Jo asks. It's the exact question Henry had.

"Nothing has changed in *one minute*. You have *always* been spell breakers! I just couldn't tell you yet. Everyone has to be the right age, of course. We were waiting for Henry to have his birthday."

"I had a birthday?"

"Yesterday. You didn't get my gift?"

Two images float up in Henry's mind like dead fish in a river: His mother, with an open box of Gingerpop Glories on her lap, licking the tips of her fingers with loud smacking sounds. His father, tossing a hardback book into the open flames of the barbecue, watching the blaze. "No. My mother and father—"

"Big, I told you." The Beautiful Librarian tsk-tsks with her finger. "You should have waited until we saw him."

"Ugh. You were right as always, my darling. Well, regardless. The best gift is the one that comes today." Grandfather lifts his glass in a toast. "Happy birthday, Henry."

The children lift theirs. "Happy birthday," Jo says, and Apollo says, and Pirate Girl says.

"And . . . To ridding the earth of evil."

The children reach across the table and clink. Rocco lifts his thimble and splashes pink onto the tablecloth.

"I don't mean to be rude, Captain Every. But maybe we should celebrate after we all come back alive," Pirate Girl says.

"And we definitely need a plan. How do we possibly parade Rocco in full view of Vlad Luxor? When? Where?" Jo takes a small sip of her drink.

"We don't need to go to *the tower*, do we?" Apollo asks. He and Henry look at each other. A million frightening thoughts pass between them. Henry's glad that Button has decided to lie right on top of his feet, because her warm body is a small comfort.

"A plan will present itself," Captain Every says. He pours another glass and swallows it down.

"That's all?" Pirate Girl says.

It sounds slightly rude, Henry thinks, but the truth is, he's very troubled, too.

"No, that's not *all*," Captain Every says, to Henry's relief. "A plan will present itself, and then you will follow it to great success."

"That's it?" Henry can't help himself.

"That's it!"

"I'm not so sure," Jo says.

"*I'm* sure! You are spell breakers, after all."

"Are you positive you don't have us mixed up with some other children?" Apollo sets down his glass.

"I most certainly do not."

"How are you one hundred percent certain?" Jo asks.

"Because you have the *keys*. You have the DNA!"

"What's DNA?" Pirate Girl asks.

"It's the material present in all living organisms that—" Apollo says.

"You have the bloodlines!" Grandfather interrupts with a bellow. "From one of the four families! The *stuff*. The genealogical madness that makes a trait last through the generations—a bulbous nose, a talent for dancing, a deep desire to wear hats."

"Wow!" Pirate Girl says. Henry's astonished, too.

Genealogical Madness Leading to
a Deep Desire to Wear Hats

"The stuff from long-gone relatives . . . ," Jo says, brightening a bit.

"I'm not so sure. I mean, I'm just an average boy," Apollo says, although, of course, Apollo has *never* been average.

"I promise you, you are the spell breakers of your generation. Each of you is from one of the four families with *the gene*. I could see that certain something in your eyes a mile away. I searched for it in *all* the possible children as I sipped my soup at La GreenWee and chose hunks of cheese at Creamy Dreamy Dairy. I saw the spark as each of you lifted your head from tying your shoes, or gazed up at the clock in the town square, or goo-goo gah-gahed from your bassinet. I knew who you were, but I had to wait until you were older to tell you."

"A certain something," Pirate Girl says. She sounds pleased with that idea.

"A glint, a glimmer, a brightness—oh, I have no idea how to explain it. You know it when you see it. As far as the four bloodlines, well, you don't have to take my word for it! Just ask your parents about your family trees, as well as the family bushes and shrubs, flora and fauna, annuals and perennials—"

"Wait. *Each* generation? Does this mean our parents are spell breakers, too?" Apollo asks.

"Heavens no! DNA is a complicated and unpredictable recipe! *All* genes are the most magical and mysterious thing on earth, let alone this one. It can hide in the parents altogether, only to—*ta-da!*—show up in the child. One year . . . What was it? Oh, the date hardly matters, but a set of twins arrived! In your parents' generation, well, it was your father's first cousin, Marcus Marc." Grandfather nods to Apollo. "Also, your aunt Maria Fernanda," he says to Jo.

"Really? My aunt Maria Fernanda?"

"Beautiful name, isn't it?" Grandfather says. "Quite musical. It skipped right through the Everys in your parents' generation, Henry. Recessive genes have their own plan, now, don't they? Your father has it," he says to Pirate Girl.

"He does?"

Pirate Girl looks stunned. She lives with her father in a house in a large field down a long, empty road. He often goes on long trips for his work, leaving her alone for days. Henry has seen him in town, head down, hands shoved in his pockets, barely speaking. He seems like the most unlikely spell breaker ever.

"Well, none of them *know*. I suppose your father will now," he says to Pirate Girl. "But there was *no need* to trouble them with that life-changing information, not with Best Farriver as our RM. Let them mow their lawns and fry their eggs in peace, I decided. We went along like that, in blissful ignorance and harmony, until a new generation was born. I identified you—four particular children, very close in age, what a miracle! And as you grew, the abilities of Cousin Marcus Marc and Aunt Maria Fernanda and Pirate Girl's father trickled away, same as hair thins on a head, or eyesight dims. Same as once-hardy dads begin to get injured every time they try to play a sport. Meanwhile, *your* abilities rose, just as nature intended."

"And then you-know-who arrived," The Beautiful Librarian says. She sets a large dish of cookies with sprinkles on the table, plucks one from it, and takes a bite.

"Since you're so close in age, I decided to wait to tell you together. Trust me, it's better not to get big news like this alone. And then Henry had his birthday, and a brother was horribly altered, and a mother was in tears. It was time."

"Our parents knew this might happen to us?" Apollo says. Poor Apollo looks betrayed. "Why didn't they say something?"

"These are not matters for the smallest small children! Would you tell your innocent, gurgling, spit-uppy brother Otto that he might have to fight great evil? Of course not! Well, he might have to, I haven't gotten a truly good look at him yet."

"Otto?" Apollo's eyes get even larger.

"And why worry a child needlessly? He or she may end up having a perfectly normal life—pruning hedges, redecorating the living room, scurrying around doing all the things grown-ups think are important at the time."

"But they must have seen the certain something in my eyes."

"Don't be ridiculous. Only I—"

"Big!" The Beautiful Librarian interrupts. "The clock! The

minutes are flying by. Tell them the story. Tell them how you *really* know all this."

"Yes, yes! Of course!" Grandfather says. He smiles at The Beautiful Librarian as if he can't imagine life without her. "Well, a long time ago, Mr. Walden Thackaray had been turned into a lizard."

"What?" Henry says.

"And I turned him back into a man."

CHAPTER 12

Mr. Thackaray and the Trip to Borneo

Henry nearly knocks over his drink. He grips the edge of the old table to steady himself. Even Button startles to her feet. This is shocking information. Clearly, the people of the province revere his grandfather. On the rare, rare days that his parents allowed it, when Henry walked with the captain along those stone streets, his small hand in his grandfather's large, warm one, he saw it— the way they'd tip their hats to him. The way they'd meet the captain's eyes and smile shyly. The way they'd refuse payment for everything from meat to milk, even though his grandfather insisted, sliding the bills across the counter firmly.

And he also saw all the gifts that would appear on his grandfather's white porch on a regular basis: a dartboard one week, a book of poetry the next. A roast beef. A deck of playing cards. A canoe. The gifts stacked up, peeking from beneath the beds and tumbling out of closets. Once, when

Henry went to retrieve his coat, he was almost struck by a small bust of Alexander the Great.

But Henry always assumed that his grandfather got the gifts and the admiration because of the captain's great intelligence and bravery at sea. He never asked why everyone in town was so respectful and generous. The gifts *had* seemed a bit strange, but it was the kind of strange that seemed like a shut door, and when a door is shut like that, you know you shouldn't ask questions. Interesting or frightening or exciting things are behind doors like that. In other words: *secrets*. And now it's as if the door is open and the secrets are tumbling out, same as Alexander the Great.

A Small Bust of Alexander the Great

"*You* are a spell breaker?" he asks.

"Holy guacamole," Pirate Girl says.

"Is that why you're always getting presents?" Henry asks.

"Oh, those. Just offerings of thanks and gratitude for the things I've done in the past. Always appreciated, I might add," Grandfather says.

"Kissing up," The Beautiful Librarian says, pouring herself

another glass of Pink Mebiolo and then passing the bottle around.

"My mother only said that you were wise. Wiser than anyone else," Jo says.

"Mine, too," Apollo says.

"I told you, these are not matters for tiny baby ears, delicate as orchid petals! And now, with Vlad Luxor as our HRM, even adults must be careful not to go around recklessly speaking of such things with each other."

"You're a spell breaker." Henry still can't believe it.

"Well, I can't break one now. I'm past my prime! The only things I can break are a hip and a promise. Still, as the oldest spell breaker alive, it's my job to identify, inform, and guide the next generation."

"That's why you called us here," Jo says.

"Indeed."

"Is that why you get to live in this magnificent place?" Pirate Girl asks, sipping her drink and reaching for a second cookie with sprinkles.

"Well, the lighthouse has always been home to an Every. My father lived here, and before him, my grandfather, a senior spell breaker himself."

"Will *my* father live here?" Henry asks.

"Never! Not in a million years."

"Why not?" Henry asks.

"Sometimes, in a family line, there's a bad seed," Grandfather says.

"A bad seed?"

"Yes. A big meanie. A tyrant. A bully who can't see or hear anything but his own needs. Who tricks others into believing they're powerless, using lies and brute force.

A Bad Seed

Unwilling to let a grandfather like me even visit a grandson like you, Henry. Not a Horrible Ruler with Magic, just a horrible human being, with everyday evil that no spell breaker can undo. Now, *those* are the people I'd like to see turned into spiders and worms and reptiles."

Grandfather is looking only at Henry now. He puts his big paw of a hand over Henry's, and Henry's throat closes up as if he might cry. His chest blooms with yearning, and it's one of those times you feel so many things that you can't say anything. Henry only nods.

Grandfather squeezes Henry's hand and leans back in his chair again and sighs. "Genes are magical *and* terrible. Unfortunately, our great-great-plus-more-greats-grandfather, the original Henry Every, was the worst bad seed of all."

"He was?"

"Pirates aren't generally the finest people."

"You're related to a *pirate*?" Pirate Girl's eyes get wide. Cookie crumbs dot her leather vest.

"Ah, yes, he is. That was a dark period in our family

history. But we come from a *long* line of explorers of the sea, many of whom were good spell break—"

"Big," The Beautiful Librarian interrupts.

"Yes, my darling?"

"There is so much to tell. I think we should stick to the story of Mr. Thackaray for now."

"Yes, of course." Grandfather Every strokes his big white beard. "Quite right. The story of Mr. Thackaray. In those days, a different man lived in the tower. Avar Slaven."

"Ooh. I can't bear to even hear that name." The Beautiful Librarian shudders.

"And before him, there was Dread Quill, and Cad Devon, and Gradion Fortrex—"

"There has never been a shortage of evil," The Beautiful Librarian adds.

"Salmon Raspuke, Trekton Miserly, Gastric Von Smite—"

"Big," The Beautiful Librarian interrupts. "Mr. Thackaray."

"Was Mr. Thackaray turned into a lizard in the Always Open Grocery?" Jo asks.

"Oh no, no, no," Grandfather says. "It happened right out there." He points. They can all see the stretch of sand that meets the shore, where there's only one lone seagull, staring out to sea.

One Lone Seagull,
Staring Out to Sea

"I saw it happen with my own eyes. I was fourteen at the time, and I was just about to step into the water for a swim. Avar Slaven had very recently moved into the tower after the grisly demise of Dread Quill. The beach was packed with people. Families having picnics. Children running into the surf. Sand making every bathing suit feel scratchy, and every sandwich crunchy. Mr. Thackaray lay out on a towel. Mrs. Thackaray lay stretched under a large beach umbrella."

"This sounds nothing like Rocco trying to get attention," Apollo says.

"Oh, it is. It's nearly the same spell, be assured. Mr. Thackaray posed with his big belly to the sky, because he was sure he looked amazing. He leaned on one elbow to show his width to his best advantage. He attempted to accidentally-on-purpose get into the background of every photograph. He strutted to the sea so that everyone might admire the arc of his middle, and then emerged from the water, proud as a great, glistening walrus."

A Great, Glistening Walrus

"Yuck," Jo says.

"And then, he began a game of beach volleyball. He served. He lunged. He spiked. However, he was the only one playing. Everyone stopped to stare. And just like that, poof! Holding an enormous volleyball was a tiny lizard wearing only a sunhat."

"Oh no," Henry says.

"There were gasps. Mrs. Thackaray began to wail. People gathered their towels and fled, leaving their sandy sandwiches half eaten on the beach, and their castle moats half filled, and their playmates half buried. Much like now, people were too afraid to return, to be in public where the eyes of evil men might be upon them. The beach remained empty. Avar Slaven had arrived, and he did *not* like the attention on anyone else but him."

"It was a dreadful time in the Timeless Province, much as it is today," The Beautiful Librarian says.

"What did you do?" Henry asks.

"I was in a predicament. Only days before, my very sick grandfather had brought me into the library to deliver the same news that you got today. He'd already informed Antonia Dante and the others—"

"Antonia Dante! My grandmother!" Apollo interrupts.

"But he wanted to protect me as long as possible. He wanted to wait until the last possible moment. And the last possible moment was exactly right then, because, in a shuddering gasp . . . Deceased!"

"Deceased?" Pirate Girl asks.

"Dead. As a doornail. Kaput. Gone. Out of here." The Beautiful Librarian snaps her fingers, as if to say *just like that.*

"I was several years over the age where I should have

been told I was a spell breaker. I understood why my grandfather wanted to keep this from me, but it left me terribly unprepared. And there I was, standing on that beach, staring at the horror that had just occurred, without his support and instruction. Alone. Never having even *met* the others. Having heard only the brief mention of their names. I didn't know what to do about Mr. Thackaray. I only knew I had to do something. I could feel that it was up to me. I felt this as sure as I felt the waves rising below my grandfather's ships during the times we'd been out to sea. It was my *duty*.

"So I left the beach and ran as fast as I could to the lighthouse library, and without even shaking the sand from my shoes, I hurried up the circular staircase. I opened the book my grandfather had showed me just before he kicked the bucket. And I read. And read. I found the answer. Breaking the spell would require a trip to Borneo, a frightening ritual with too many orangutans, and coconut on two separate occasions. Even though I was frightened and had no idea what lay ahead, I was ready. I learned—as we all do in terrible times—who I really *am*. I felt it *here*." Grandfather thumps his large chest.

"I went back to the beach to ponder a plan, with eyes that had newly been opened. And then, right outside, I saw it. A ship. My grandfather's ship. It was there like an answer to my question, as if he were here to help me after all. I realized at once that I had to sail it to Borneo to break the spell."

"Can *we* sail a ship to Borneo instead of facing Vlad Luxor?" Pirate Girl asks.

"Oh no. This is *Lizardo Nakedismo*. Mr. Thackaray was wearing a sunhat. Besides, that ship was wrecked in a storm on the voyage across the sea. Broken into a million pieces. I had to swim to shore, clutching a bit of planking, wearing only my striped bathing trunks, popular at the time."

Striped Bathing Trunks, Popular at the Time

"Your poor ship," Pirate Girl says.

"Poor *you*," Jo says with her usual thoughtfulness. "What happened then?"

"Well, as the spell breaking required, there was a ritual with a troop of orangutans, involving a large snake, a few feathers, and a coconut."

"That sounds terrifying," Apollo says.

"Not half as terrifying as the giant *mosquito humongo* who bit a chunk out of my leg, right through the mosquito netting above my bed. I still have the scar. Unfortunately, this particular bug was carrying malaria, which resulted in a jungle fever, bizarre hallucinations, and rivers of sweat. I wasn't sure I'd survive."

"Oh no," Henry says.

"I fought a torrid delirium and the black rumbling of thunder in my lower guts. Finally, the fever lifted. I was too weak to continue, however, and so I caught a cargo ship and returned home, the spell unbroken."

"How discouraging," Jo says.

"And yet delicious. It was a cargo ship of coconuts."

"Yum," Pirate Girl says.

"And that was when, much to my surprise and delight, I got a telegram from Antonia Dante, saying that the lizard had turned back into Mr. Thackaray. I knew my efforts had paid off. Coconut on two separate occasions! I had the *stuff*. And so do you. I had a *duty*. And so do you." Captain Every looks at each of them, until his eyes land on Henry. "I had the ability to be much more than I ever thought I could be."

All of the cookies have vanished from the plate, nervously eaten same as the Dante children devour a bowl of Kernel Krispy Pops during a particularly nail-biting episode of *Rocket Galaxy*. Apollo's cheeks are flushed with excitement. Pirate Girl's eyes are practically dancing. Jo sits with her arms folded in determination. Even Button and Rocco have been listening, animal chins up and ears alert. And Henry feels different from how he did when he first heard the news, too. When his grandfather looks at him like that, he feels that little flickery flame again.

"That's a very inspiring story, Captain Every," Jo says, putting it perfectly.

"I'm so excited to have a duty," Pirate Girl says.

"Of course, this doesn't mean that I didn't nearly lose my life on numerous occasions. And if Vlad Luxor ever learns you exist, there will be many more reasons to be afraid."

"Big. Don't scare the children," The Beautiful Librarian says, most definitely scaring the children.

"Spell breaking requires great courage," Grandfather reminds them. "You will need to be alert when you are drowsy. Aware when you are distracted. There will be many great dangers and difficulties."

Rocco waves his little thimble for more pink juice. "Urp," he burps, as loudly as possible.

"Like hiding in plain sight when your naked lizard loves to monster belch."

"Say 'excuse me,' Rocco," Apollo says.

"Excuse me, Rocco," Rocco says in his tiny voice.

"What do we do next?" Henry asks.

"You look," Grandfather says. "You seek more information. You listen. You try to understand. You see with new eyes. And the answers to your questions will appear."

CHAPTER 13
Henry Returns to His Hideous Home

On the ride home, the children stop at the Circle of the Y. Button hops out of Pirate Girl's sidecar. Rocco pops his head from Apollo's pocket. There, with the Hollow Valley and the Wilds in front of them, and the Jagged Mountains beyond that, with the road down to the sea on one side, and the road up Rulers Mountain on the other, it seems like they've already gone through something together. Something large and very important.

All of them feel this, Henry knows. He can tell by the way Pirate Girl gets off her bike, unsnaps her helmet, and takes it off. And how Jo takes hers off, as well, in no hurry to leave just yet. Apollo's expression is serious. They can feel it all around them—the deep knowing that much more is to come. Before today, too, Henry felt mostly just lonely, like the one strange fish among the other fish. But now, in spite of the terrible troubles ahead, he feels the new possibility of belonging.

Jo tucks her hair behind her ears, in a way that means an important moment has arrived. She puts her clasped hands in front of her. "Everybody in," she says.

Apollo piles his hands on top, and then Pirate Girl does, and so does Henry. Henry has seen other children do this on the playground. In the movies they watch at school, it also happens whenever a sports team has no

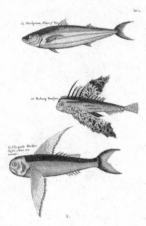

The One Strange Fish Among the Other Fish

chance of winning. He always wished that his hands might be in a stack like that one day, and it's just as warm and wonderful as he imagined. Standing all together, with this dazzling flowering meadow around them, he *believes* in magic. At least, he's trying very hard to believe, with the tower still looming within sight, its shadow growing even larger as the day goes on. Henry tries not to look up there.

Pirate Girl is also aware of that tower. She scans their surroundings before she speaks. "Spell breakers," she says, oh so quietly.

"Spell breakers," Apollo and Jo and Henry repeat with a whisper.

"Doo-doo breakers," Rocco shouts, his little reptile head sticking out from his brother's pocket.

"Oh, Rocco!" Apollo moans. "You're going to get us *all* turned into naked lizards!"

"Should we meet here tomorrow?" Henry asks. After this whole, incredible day, an unfamiliar confidence is rising in him. At least, it's there if he keeps his eyes away from that shadow.

"Tomorrow," they agree.

They pedal back through the meadow, and at the edge of town, at the very spot where they'll go their separate ways, they stop once more.

"Come here, Button," Henry says, and the dog hops out of Pirate Girl's sidecar.

"Bye, Button. See you soon," Pirate Girl says.

"It's weird. But I don't want to leave you guys," Jo says.

Henry knows just what she means. He's too embarrassed to say anything like that back, so he just pats her shoulder awkwardly, until she leans forward and hugs each of them quickly before pedaling off.

Henry watches the shiny stream of Josephine Idár's hair falling down her serious back as she rides into town. Jo lives with her mother, Isabelle, and two little sisters, Luna and Lola, in an apartment above Rio Royale, where Jo's mother is owner and head chef. Henry's seen Jo through the window of the restaurant, doing her homework in romantic lighting at an elegant table, underneath the huge painting of a fancy fox.

Jo's mother works so hard that Henry has also seen Jo

The Huge Painting of a Fancy Fox

taking care of her sisters, zipping their jackets, holding their hands as they cross the street. It must be a heavy burden sometimes, watching others like that.

"My turn," Pirate Girl says. She snaps her helmet back on.

"Bye, Pirate Girl," Henry says.

Pirate Girl waves as she disappears down the cobblestones, and they wave back. After she rides through town, Pirate Girl will have to bump down the dirt road to the house in the field where she and her father live. Sometimes, in the winter, that field is covered with enormous sheets of ice, which Pirate Girl must cross all by herself to get to school. He remembers other things about her now, too—how some of the kids call her names until Apollo tells them to stop. How, on the days Pirate Girl packs her own lunch, he's seen Jo trying to give *her* half a sandwich, same as she does for Henry. For the first time, he wonders if Pirate Girl is ever as lonely as he is.

Henry and Apollo head to their own street now. When they finally reach Apollo's huge house, which sits next to Henry's small and leaning one, Apollo gets off his bike again.

"Hey, Henry?" he says. "Thank you for helping us. Thank you *tons*."

Henry right then . . . Well, his insides gush up with feeling, like a glorious fountain. He wants to hug Apollo right around the middle and squeeze him so hard that his eyes pop. He wants to soar like an eagle, or slay a dangerous dragon in the name of friendship. He tries for something more dignified and suitable to the occasion.

"Hey, no problem," he says with a shrug.

Apollo and Rocco disappear through their front door. Henry can smell the smells of Meat Magnifique and Gravy drifting deliciously from the Dante house. He misses everyone already.

After this day, it's hard, very hard, to do what he must do next.

Henry goes home.

CHAPTER 14

A New Disaster

As soon as Henry shuts the front door behind him, he and Button discover that the beer can chicken has already been eaten. The boiled potatoes are gone. Even the last magenta, dirt-flavored beet has vanished. Button's eyes look as sad as Henry's.

"Where have you been?" his father snarls the moment he sees him. "Out playing with your friends? It must be nice to be a child who is given everything and does nothing in return. When I was your age, I worked my bones to the ground every day at the shipyard."

"You never worked a day in your life," his mother snaps to his father. "And you," she says, pointing at Henry. "You left without cleaning your room. It's a pigsty."

"I'm sorry," Henry says.

"No television for a week," his father says, from in front of the TV.

"All right." Henry nods, his head down. He's never allowed to watch television anyway.

"And what is the meaning of leaving this trash outside?" His mother waves Henry's treasured *Ranger Scout Handbook*, which he left under the bush for safekeeping. "Do

A Pigsty

you think it's polite or respectful to just leave your junk anywhere you wish?" She presses the silver pedal of the garbage can and the lid pops up. She tosses the handbook inside. "No television, *and* you are grounded for *two* weeks. You will not leave this house, Henry Every. Sloppy, ungrateful boys must be punished. Selfish little brats need to think about something other than *themselves.*"

Henry's stomach hurts. His heart hurts, too, for his beloved book now lying among coffee grounds and canned beet juice and chicken bones. He's hungry and exhausted, and now he's also very worried. Grounded! What will happen tomorrow, when the children meet at the Circle of the Y and he never shows up? This is a disaster.

When Henry's sure his parents are asleep, he tiptoes downstairs. He listens for any creaks on the stairs or squeaks of bedsprings. He finds an apple and a plate of chicken, hidden far back in the vegetable bin. He steps on the metal lever of the garbage can and takes the *Ranger Scout Handbook*, sixth edition, out from the trash. He wipes its cover clean.

Upstairs, Henry eats the apple. He gives the chicken to Button. She's been a good dog and a real friend. She overcame her worst impulses and didn't eat a scurrying creature. She ran a great distance, and was quite patient with an annoying naked lizard. She led the way right beside Henry.

As he eats, Henry sits on his bed and looks through his book and tries to find a way out of his current problem. Button lies beside him, panting a calm and steady *huh uh huh uh huh*. His grandfather said that there would be answers when they needed answers, and so Henry hunts for them. *How to send silent signals.* No. *How to identify poison plants.* No. *How to live the Scout ideals. How to measure the length of your step. How to stalk a herd of grazing deer. How to make a bear-claw necklace.* No, no, no, and no.

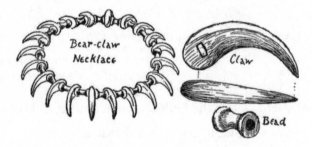

How to Make a Bear-Claw Necklace

Henry misses his grandfather with such an ache that there are no words for it. He misses Apollo and Jo and Pirate Girl. He sets his cheek on Button's soft side and listens to her heartbeat. His head goes up and down with her breathing.

He feels a pain at the center of his chest, where every human being feels longing.

It's almost impossible not to believe the lies people tell you about yourself. Henry wants to cry. It's like all the magic of the day has vanished. He gets up from his bed. He opens his window and leans out. The moon is big, and the summer air is cool. He listens for any noises at the Dante house. But no one is laughing tonight.

CHAPTER 15

A Lizard's Plea

Well, it was a long and sleepless night for Henry, as you can imagine. But now, after the summer sun has risen once again, he hears Apollo out on his front lawn, calling toward Henry's open window.

"Henry! Come *on*! Where *are* you?"

Henry wants to fold his thin, featherless pillow over his head. Button sits beside his bed and stares at him like she has serious matters to discuss. People who think dogs don't talk are wrong, Henry's sure. Talking does not always need words.

"Okay, okay," he says to Button.

He leans out the window. He's afraid to say what he has to say. Henry hates disappointing people.

"I can't come."

"What do you mean, you can't come? You have to come!" Apollo is wearing a pair of summer shorts and a new T-shirt that gleams in the morning sun. He has a backpack on his back. Rocco stands upright on Apollo's shoulder, balancing on one foot, his little lizard arms out like a magnificent tightrope walker. He's going to break his neck.

"I'm grounded."

"How can you be grounded? You never do anything wrong!"

"It's a long story."

Apollo paces. "Henry. We *need* you. We can't do this without you."

It seems incredible, doesn't it? It is to him—to be a normal boy who suddenly finds himself necessary. The small, bright flame is there again. It fills Henry with a cautious flicker of courage.

A Magnificent Tightrope Walker

"Okay. Let me see what I can do."

He'll sneak out even if he is grounded, that's what he can do. Oh, it'll be dangerous. He's never done anything like that before. He tucks Button under his arm. At his door, he listens. He hears the television downstairs, and his mother's voice. And then he hears quite a few crashes and bangs. He opens his door a tiny bit and peeks out, and immediately, his spirits sink and his courage evaporates.

There's a bunch of stuff blocking his exit. His mother is cleaning out her closet, and objects are flying out of her bedroom and forming a mountain in the hallway. There are skis, and there's a barbell, and there are tracksuits in various colors, all unworn. There are dinner jackets, and there's a briefcase and an ancient calculator.

It's like a big pile of good intentions gone wrong. A book, *Vegetarian Cooking for the New Millennium*, soars through the air and lands with a *thunk* on the pile.

"None of this, none of this, none of this!" his mother shouts. "Useless trash, pointless garbage!"

"What's that, Mrs. Every?" his father shouts over the TV.

"You never hear a word I say!" she shouts back.

What was he thinking? Of course he can't do something bold and dangerous like this! Henry returns to the window. "It's hopeless," he tells Apollo.

"Can't you just explain things to your parents?" Apollo asks, proving that he'll never understand. When Henry thinks of explaining things to his parents, he imagines the cover of one of his favorite comic books in the school library: *Kona, Monarch of Monster Isle*.

"It's no use."

"You can't be defeated yet! We haven't even faced Vlad Luxor!"

Kona, Monarch of Monster Isle

Right there, stuck in his room, Henry wonders if Vlad Luxor might be easier to deal with than his mother and father.

"Remember what your grandfather said? You're supposed to be brave, Henry." Apollo looks like he's about to cry again. His face wrinkles up like an old Kleenex. His eyes get watery. He sniffs a truly long and—ew, so sorry for these details—juicy sniff. Oh, it's awful.

"Wait," Apollo says, his voice wobbly. "What's that, Rocco? Just a sec. Rocco's trying to tell me something." Apollo holds his little brother up close to his ear, listens, and nods.

"Rocco says . . . 'Please, Henry. You have *the stuff.'*"

"Oh, Rocco . . . ," Henry sighs.

"He's *begging*."

Ugh! It feels impossible. If Henry defies his parents, they'll stand over him, gnashing their big T. rex teeth and reaching with their tiny T. rex arms. But if he obeys, Rocco will be a lizard forever, and more terrible things will happen to small children and grandmothers and science teachers and other innocent people.

It's very difficult to believe what his grandfather told him, about having the ability to be more than he thinks he can be. It's hard to imagine that he even has the *s* or the *t*, let alone all of *the stuff*.

He squinches his eyes tight. He tries very hard to feel that flame again. He concentrates, until there it is—the small burn of courage. It's funny, but in that flame, he almost sees his very own self, his truest self, very far away but waving his arms as if to say, *Over here, Henry.*

All right. He'll let luck determine his fate, Henry decides in an instant. He opens his *Ranger Scout Handbook* randomly, and looks at the page to see if there's an answer.

The index. No! Try again.

How to make a bedsheet into a rope.

Henry smiles.

"Prepare my bike," Henry says to Apollo.

CHAPTER 16
An Astonishing Escape

Henry's heart is pounding with nerves. He strips the sheet from the bed while listening carefully for any sound that his mother might be coming. He twists and knots the sheet according to the diagram. He ties one end to a corner of the metal bedpost, and yanks to test the strength. Pretty good, actually.

Henry's not sure if it's his imagination, but the house goes quiet. His mother has stopped yelling. Things are not crashing onto the pile. His father must have turned down the sound with the remote.

He can practically hear the pulse of his own blood in his veins.

He'd better hurry. And he'd better be absolutely silent. Henry puts his finger to his lips to make sure that Apollo doesn't make a sound. Rocco puts a tiny lizard finger to his own lips. *Please, Rocco,* Henry thinks. *Please be a calm and well-behaved naked lizard for five minutes.*

Henry shoves his *Ranger Scout Handbook* into the

farthest corner of his closet where it won't be found. At the last second, he grabs his lucky marble and stuffs it into his pocket, because he'll need all the luck he can get. Finally, Henry scoops up Button. Oh dear, oh dear—he didn't think this through. It's going to be tricky, very tricky, to climb down a rope using one hand while gripping a wriggly Jack Russell terrier with the other.

You already know that one should never try this at home, of course. Never, ever, ever. These are dire and drastic measures, used only when fighting great evil.

Henry climbs over the ledge. Apollo seemed so close a minute ago, but now he looks a hundred miles away. Henry doesn't feel like he has *the stuff*. Not at all. Not by a long shot.

It's too, too quiet in the house. Something's wrong. He needs to speed this up.

Henry grips the rope and scoots from the ledge. Once it's in his hands, Henry is reminded that the rope is not a rope at all, but a thin, worn bedsheet. He hangs in midair. His skinny legs dangle. Still, Henry feels like he's the Great Kellar, performing one of his most astonishing feats.

The Great Kellar, Performing One of His Most Astonishing Feats

It feels amazing, and terrifying, but . . . He's doing it! He's making his way to the ground! Poor Button's belly is being squeezed, and she's squirming and twisting around when she must *not* squirm and twist around. Henry's trying to grip her as he edges down the bedsheet rope, when suddenly, he thinks he hears the bed slide just a little.

He stops and listens.

Screeech. The slight scrape of metal against wood.

"Come on, come on!" Apollo says.

"Henry?" his mother calls.

Oh no!

"Henry, what are you doing in there?"

He edges. The bed scoots again.

SCREEECH. Now there's a small screaming sound as the metal feet of the bed very definitely skate across the wood floor.

"Henry! What's that noise?" his mother shouts.

"Hurry!" Apollo whispers. Rocco is jumping up and down on his shoulder, either from excitement or because he has to go to the bathroom quite badly.

Henry's almost there. His feet are nearly on the ground, when suddenly, with a terrible, terrible racket, with a smash, crash, and clatter, the bed slides all at once.

BAM!

It bangs against the window, and the metal bed frame smacks the glass, which cracks and shatters to a zillion pieces. A beautiful hailstorm of clear crystals showers over him.

"HENRY EVERY!" his mother screams.

"Oh no, oh no, oh NO!" Henry whispers.

He leaps the last few feet down, tumbles to the grass. Button wriggles free. Apollo has Henry's bike upright and waiting for him.

"Go," Apollo says.

CHAPTER 17

The Surprise in the Backpack

Henry rides like the wind. Ahead of him, Apollo pedals as fast as he can. Then, Apollo lets go of both handlebars and pumps his fists in the air with victory. He shouts something over his shoulder that must be, "Way to go, Henry!" but sounds more like *Ay O, Nree!* once it travels through the breeze and reaches Henry's ears.

Henry doesn't feel quite as triumphant. He can't believe what he's just done. It's possible he may never be able to go home again. As they bump along the cobblestones of town and cross onto the dirt path of the meadow, Henry scrolls through his options. He and Button may have to live in a train car, riding the rails forever. He may have to join a circus, and Button may have to learn various humiliating tricks.

Henry may have to go live at his grandfather's house.

Well, he knows that will never happen, no matter what terrible thing he does. His mother and father hate Grandfather Every. They spew venom at his kindness and spit on

Various Humiliating Tricks

his every attempt at showing care. They're jealous of the lighthouse and the gifts and the way the people love him and—Henry understands this now—they're jealous he's a senior spell breaker. They despise *everything* Grandfather has that they don't, which also includes Henry's heart. So they keep Henry from him, and every visit or basket of food is arranged in secret, allowed in a random fashion, or forbidden with fury. The things his grandfather said about randomness and fury are things Henry understands from personal experience.

Still, the thought of living with his grandfather at the lighthouse fills Henry with a . . . Well, do you know the kind of hope that is so magnificent and magical and *hopeful* that you don't even dare to think about it? The kind of hope that feels like it's made of the brightest warm light? *That* is what he's filled with. With every swivel of the lantern, the lighthouse says, *Blink, there's a safe place in the world. Blink, you won't be lost forever. Blink, you are never as alone as you feel.*

No hopeful daydreams matter right at that moment, though, because the truth is, he's in big, big trouble. The biggest he's ever been in. Pirate Girl may have broken her arm, and Apollo once broke his mother's garden-gnome music box, but Henry has never broken anything. Of course, he's gotten into trouble plenty of times from his parents, but he's never actually done anything wrong. Now he's shattered a window and made an escape. He can't even imagine what he'll face when he goes back.

All of this thinking makes him suddenly feel weak. And wobbly. And woozy. He feels like a soap bubble about to pop. "Wait up!" he calls to Apollo, who's gotten so far ahead that he's a small spot in that field full of dandelions and forget-me-nots.

Henry stops his bike. He doesn't feel well at all. He could keel right over. Apollo loops back and makes a screeching arc in front of Henry's bike that sends meadow dirt flying.

"Are you okay?"

"I don't know. I . . ."

"Maybe you need a snack," Apollo says. "My mother always gives me a snack when I look like that."

Food, Henry thinks. He has barely eaten anything since the meal at his grandfather's house.

Apollo swings his backpack off. He unzips it.

And Henry—well, he can't believe his eyes.

Inside, there are Monster Munchies, and Rainbow Target Pops. There are Salt-Freckled Zappers, and Jam Giants. And, oh heavens, there are Yummers With Cheese, *and* Yummers Without Cheese! There are squishy pockets of the juice of every fruit, and there's even a red plaid thermos of chocolate milk with a cup on top.

"I haven't eaten since yesterday," Henry says.

"You haven't?" Apollo's eyes get wide. "Why not? That's crazy. Well, eat up, Henry. Eat all you want. There's plenty for everyone."

It's weird how sometimes the worst day can turn *just like that* into the best one. (Though, right then, Henry has forgotten that it can turn *just like that* back into the worst again.)

"Is it really all right?" he says, before he reaches for a Yummer With Cheese.

"Of course! Why wouldn't it be? Have them all if you want, Henry. Give some to Button, too."

Oh, oh, oh! He peels the foil and sinks his teeth into the buttery, gooey-ooey deliciousness. They are as magnificent as he ever imagined. They melt on his tongue, and send jolts of joy through him after he swallows. The cheese stretches to impossible lengths. He gives pieces to Button, who downs them in one gulp. He feels glorious, because he is eating and drinking, slurping packages of mandarin-kumquat juice *and* kumquat-mandarin. His tummy is getting full and Button's tummy is likely getting full, too, and he can see the Y in the road ahead, not nearly as far as it felt before.

"Better, Henry?"

"Much."

"You just needed a snack," Apollo says, and zips his pack. "Onward?"

"Onward."

As if the day couldn't get more fabulous, Henry spots the shining hair of Jo Idár, flowing like a beautiful waterfall from her bike helmet, as she waits in the Circle of the Y.

A Beautiful Waterfall

Pirate Girl's there, too, kicking the dirt with her boot. She's wearing her pants with lots of pockets, and the pockets seem to be stuffed with a million things. Her sidecar is overflowing.

"Took you guys long enough," she says.

CHAPTER 18

An Encounter with
Needleman and the Squirrel

Apollo puts his kickstand down. Jo clicks her helmet over her handlebars. Henry shakes a pebble from his shoe.

"Um," Pirate Girl says. "What happens now?"

And, oh wow, this is awkward, because they all look toward Henry. He has no idea what to do next. He starts to panic a little. His thoughts become a useless bunch of belches and farts. And then, all at once, thank heavens, some words form and fly out of his mouth like a mostly orderly flock of geese.

"We'll have a meeting."

A Mostly Orderly Flock of Geese

"A meeting!" Jo nods, as if it's a terrific idea.

Apollo looks doubtful. "My father has lots of those at work, and he says they're a waste of time."

"Manuela Sáenz had *lots* of meetings with high-ranking military officers to discuss the revolutions in Latin America. And so did my mother, after she bought Rio Royale from Mr. Swinehoff."

"Wait. Is it safe here?" Pirate Girl asks.

She's right. It's easy to forget. They glance around, their heads swiveling. How can you tell who is who and what is what, though? Every spider is a possible spy of Vlad Luxor's. Every crow might be a gossip. Every rock might not be a rock. That tree could be the missing Dr. Indigo Evans, who vanished one day when she was helping the wounded Bartleby family, who'd been injured during that terrible windstorm. Vlad believes that people should help only themselves.

"Are we safe anywhere?" Henry asks.

"Good point," Apollo says.

"We'll sit close together and keep our voices low," Jo says.

They plop on the grass in a circle, with Button in the middle. Rocco is curled on top of the dog's soft head. An ant makes a determined trek over the mountain of Henry's ankle. His stomach aches with the weight of leadership.

"All right," he says.

There's a painful moment of silence. Henry hears a large

clock ticking in his head. Pirate Girl picks grass and piles it into a mound.

"Okay, I know something important," Jo says, saving Henry's skin. "We should definitely talk about what happened last night."

"What happened last night?" Apollo asks.

"Yeah, what happened last night?" Pirate Girl says.

"You guys didn't hear? Vlad Luxor turned Mrs. Trembly into a yellow-beaked starling! My mother told me."

"Oh no!" Henry says. "That's terrible!" Mrs. Trembly is the school librarian. Henry loves her. He can't imagine more awful news.

"She didn't even *do* anything. Vlad Luxor just doesn't approve of the books on her shelves. Too much knowledge isn't good for the people."

"That's ridiculous," Pirate Girl whispers.

A Yellow-Beaked Starling

"It was bad. Very bad. She was in her own garden, staring at the moon through her telescope, when *bam*. Now the only thing she can say is *caw, caw, caw*."

"He's *got* to be stopped." Yummers With Cheese plus this tragic news have renewed Henry's determination.

"And another important thing. I asked my mother about Aunt Maria Fernanda," Jo continues. "She said it was true, what Captain Every said. And then she held my hands and very quietly asked, 'You?' and I nodded. My mother cried and then kissed me on both cheeks and told me she was proud. She told me that the women of my family had been fighters against injustice all the way back to Manuela Sáenz, revolutionary hero of South America."

"Wow." To Henry, this sounds so much more important than a family of pirates and *bad seeds*.

"I asked my dad," Apollo says. "I didn't tell him about me yet, though. My parents are already upset enough about Rocco. But Dad said that we came from a long line of great thinkers and philosophers."

"What's a philosopher?" Pirate Girl asks.

"Someone who thinks smart stuff and says smart stuff," Apollo says. "We also had an astronaut. An explorer of the wide and mysterious cosmos."

"How awesome," Jo says, and fixes her eyes on Apollo.

The Wide and Mysterious Cosmos

Henry sighs. Even Apollo's relatives were handsome and smart and brave.

"I couldn't ask," Pirate Girl says. "My dad wasn't home." Pirate Girl plucks a dandelion puff and blows. The seeds drift off to create a million more dandelion puffs.

"Wait, what, Rocco?" Apollo takes Rocco from Button's head and holds him to his ear to better hear.

"Flying astronaut!" Rocco squeaks. He flaps his tiny naked lizard arms, and then he leaps from Apollo's hand.

It is a long way down for a lizard. Plus, he immediately disappears in the tall grass. In an instant, Pirate Girl spots him and snatches him right up, like a crouton from a salad.

"I guess not everyone in the family uses their head," Apollo says, plucking him from Pirate Girl's fingers. "Rocco, how will we ever get out of this alive if you keep being such a naughty, troublesome—"

But Apollo doesn't have the chance to finish. Because, right then, a giant acorn rolls across the ground and hits Apollo's shoe. The children follow the route of the acorn and look up. They gasp. A fat, sly squirrel sits beside the thin, dark figure of Mr. Needleman, Vlad Luxor's right-hand man.

Henry and Pirate Girl scurry madly to their feet. Jo and Apollo do the same. How long has Needleman been there, watching and listening? The children stand as close to each other as possible, elbows touching elbows, sneakers next to sneakers. Henry's tennis-ball knees practically knock together. Goose bumps edge up his arms. Button growls long and low, and Henry grabs her collar so she'll stop.

Needleman—he's as tall as a medium lamppost, and thin as an envelope. His nose slides down to a sharp point. His bow tie is crisp. And that squirrel looks capable of doing all of the sudden and creepy squirrel-ish things you worry a squirrel might do, like darting up your pant leg or leaping into your hair.

"Four children," Mr. Needleman says.

"Five," Rocco squeaks, too softly for Mr. Needleman to hear, fortunately.

"Four *particular* children."

"Five, five, five," Rocco says.

Apollo shoves Rocco into his pocket, where he rattles around with two quarters and a five-dollar bill. Pirate Girl takes Jo's hand, because Jo is trembling.

Henry clears his throat. It's hard to even speak in Mr. Needleman's presence.

"We were just heading to the, uh, store—" Henry croaks out a lie.

"The store."

"The Always Open."

"The Always Open is closed."

"The Always Open is never closed," Pirate Girl says.

"Well, it is now. Renovations!"

"Renovations?" Pirate Girl asks. Henry wishes she'd get that challenging look out of her eyes.

"Improvements. Sprucing up. Making things look pretty! And why were four children going alone to the store? Children should never be alone! Why have you left the protection of your cul-de-sacs and car seats and baby gates?"

Apollo thinks quickly. "Milk. My mother ran out of milk."

"And it takes four particular children to get it?" Needleman raises one eyebrow.

"She needs a very large carton," Apollo says.

"We'll just, uh, get it another time," Henry says.

"Well, remember, children. It's quite perilous out here on the road and in the city and in the valley and in the country and by the sea alone without your parents."

"We'll remember."

"It's very dangerous to be on playgrounds and on sidewalks and on bicycles. Deadly to eat sugary foods and to use butter knives and touch dirty doorknobs. Toxic to eat unwashed vegetables and unbaked cookie dough. Lethal to be out of range of baby monitors and cell phones. The only safe thing to do is hold the hands of your mommies at every moment."

Henry isn't so sure about this, but he's keeping his mouth shut.

"Onward! Off you go," Needleman says. And then he does a terrible thing. He leans forward, takes his thumb and forefinger, and flicks Henry right on his narrow knob of a shoulder.

Henry feels the little jab of pain, but this isn't what

actually hurts. He doesn't know why, but that flick makes him feel awful and ashamed.

"Come, Mr. Reese," Needleman says to the squirrel.

Needleman's jacket flaps flap as he turns and disappears down the road to town. They wait until he's out of sight.

"Mr. Reese!" Jo says, speaking barely above a whisper. "I thought that squirrel looked familiar. Needleman is Vlad Luxor's right-hand man, but Mr. Reese used to be the left. Mr. Reese was horrible! He tattled on Mr. Trevor Tinkle, one of the waiters at Rio Royale, and Vlad Luxor turned him into a humiliating statue."

"You mean that statue in the town square?" Apollo asks.

"That's the one."

"I had no idea that was Mr. Tinkle," Apollo says.

"Needleman *flicked* you," Pirate Girl says. She looks furious.

If you've ever had a bully be mean to you, you might un- derstand what Henry feels now. He feels small. He feels like

Mr. Tinkle

he's the one who did something bad. It's wrong and con- fusing, but bullies excel at the wrong and confusing.

"I want to punch his face in," Pirate Girl says. Button barks in agreement.

Rocco pops his head from Apollo's pocket. "Pow," he squeaks. He makes a little fist.

"Do you think he knows about us? Could he have heard? The way he said 'Four particular children' . . ." Apollo shudders.

"He wouldn't have just let us walk away, would he? Or else, he's running off to tell Vlad Luxor about us now," Jo says.

"I guess we'll know when we *all* get turned to lizards. Or worms, or rodents, or—"

Apollo interrupts Pirate Girl and looks at Henry. "Your grandfather said we'd see answers about what to do next, but I don't see any answers. I see only dangers." His eyes are wide, and his lips are trembling.

"Not to be disrespectful to Captain Every," Jo says. "But when Manuela Sáenz fought with the rebel army in the Battle of Junín, she did not wait for answers. She strategized. She made a plan."

The Battle of Junín

"He didn't say *wait*. He said *seek*. And *look*. And *listen*," Pirate Girl says.

"I vote to make a plan," Apollo says.

"Let's go to Rio Royale and sit under the painting of a fancy fox. We'll be safe there." Jo fastens the snap under her helmet. She looks very decisive again, now that Needleman is gone. Henry suddenly remembers from Jo's oral report that Manuela Sáenz became a lieutenant, and then a captain, and then a colonel.

Henry doesn't feel decisive, not at all. He doubts they'll be safe when they reach Rio Royale. From his long personal experience, *safety* is a sweet dream, found only in the soft folds of sleep, or in his imagination. He wishes so bad that he could believe in it. It's the most beautiful wish he has.

CHAPTER 19

A Shocking New Message

As the children ride their bikes through Huge Meadow, heading back toward town and Rio Royale, it's hard not to get that creepy feeling where you jump at every blade of grass that slips by your bare legs, and jolt at every gnat that bumps your forehead. Behind them, on Rulers Mountain, the tower rises to the sky, and the black mirrors warp and stretch every tree and cloud. The shadow is dull and cold, wide as it is long. As he rides through it, Henry feels as if he's in the freezer section of the Always Open, now closed. But this is a freezer section with only frozen vegetables, and the worst ones, too: gross blocks of spinach, little yucky cubes of carrots, disgustingly icy green beans.

It's summer, but in that dark space you

Disgustingly Icy Green Beans

can only think of winter. The sun is gone. The crows sit in the trees but say nothing. Pirate Girl rides next to Henry. In the sidecar, Button's ears are back, same as when she hears a skittering creature under the floorboards at night, and Rocco huddles close to Button's white paws. Pirate Girl pedals without terror, though. At least, her hands have a determined hold on the handlebars, and the look on her face is fierce. Henry wonders if she *ever* feels afraid.

Ahead of them, on her yellow bike, Jo leads, with Apollo right behind her. It's strange, but as he watches Apollo ride through that shadow, Henry gets a terrible feeling. A feeling of doom. For all of them, but maybe especially for Apollo.

Henry pedals harder.

They bump up onto the cobblestones of town, leaving the meadow behind them. All they have to do is reach Rio Royale, where they can make a plan.

But suddenly, this is a lot trickier than it sounds. Main Street and the town square are filled with people. Everyone in the Timeless Province seems to be there. Henry sees some of their classmates with their parents. He spots the owner of the candy store, and teachers from school, and even Jo's mother, Isabelle Idár, in the distance, wiping her hands on her apron.

"Mom!" Jo calls, but it's too noisy and crowded for her to hear. "What in the world is going on?"

"No idea. But this can't be good," Pirate Girl says. She's

jostled from behind, and Henry is shoved by a shopping bag. People are standing on their toes, trying to see.

"There's a new message on the billboard, I think," Henry says.

They maneuver through the swarm. With Button under Henry's arm and Rocco on Apollo's shoulder, the children edge and wind their way to the front of the crowd. They tilt their chins up like everyone else to read the shocking announcement:

TODAY! PARAD AND FARE! CELEBRAT THE GREAT VLAD LUXOR! YOU'RE WELCOME!

"Parad and fare?" Henry whispers. "Celebrat?"

"I think he means *parade* and *fair*," Jo says. "*Celebrate*."

"Parad and fare!" Pirate Girl snickers a dangerous snicker. "Cele*brat*!" She's about to burst with chuckles. Do you know those moments when it is the worst possible time to laugh but it begins to happen anyway? When you're being scolded, for example, or when a room is silent and serious, and a very wrong giddiness rises up and threatens to explode out of your mouth? Well, that is exactly what happens now. Pirate Girl's eyes get wide and glittery, and she makes that dangerous *ckkk* sound in the back of her throat, the sound of laughter being strangled to silence. Jo elbows her. Pirate Girl's shoulders begin to go up and down in muffled chortles. Henry doesn't dare look her way. His own bubble of hilarity is rising, threatening to erupt in a loud HAHAHA!

"Cele*brat*!" Pirate Girl snickers again and snorts.

Henry is making the *ckkk* sound now, too. He focuses on Button's collar. Apollo looks down at his shoes. Jo stares at a baby in a carriage. If any of them meet eyes, they'll *all* burst out laughing, and then the people around them will laugh, and then the whole crowd will start in, and *everyone* will get turned into statues and sparrows and trees.

Oh no! There's twittering all around. *A lot* of people are making the *ckkk* sound. *Many* shoulders are going up and down. That baby begins to gurgle with giggles. Even Button's lips are turned up in a dog smile. They have to stop, though. They *must*, because *this* kind of laughter is dangerous.

But then . . . The message changes before their very eyes. TODAY! PARADE AND FAYRE! CELEBRATE THE GREAT VLAD LUXOR! YOU'RE WELCOME! YOU DID NOT SEE THE MESSAGE THAT CAME BEFORE THIS ONE! REPEAT! YOU DID NOT SEE THE MESSAGE THAT CAME BEFORE THIS ONE!

"Fayre," Pirate Girl snickers. Jeez! She's as dangerous as Rocco!

A parade and a fair. They had these before, when Best Farriver was their RM. Men and women from Everything Storage set up games and rides, and people lined the streets, and little children sat on the shoulders of their fathers to get a better view of the parade. Between the knees of his parents in front of him, Henry could glimpse colorful floats and baton twirlers, men eating fire, and marching bands. At the fair, his parents bought two scrumptious Choco Blocks on a stick, and gave Henry the sticks. They stood in line so that his father could toss rings over the tops of bottles. They stood in another so that his mother could shoot a spray of water into a clown's mouth. His mother and father rode the very colorful race-car ride as Henry waited below.

The Very Colorful Race-Car Ride

"Parad," Pirate Girl says. She's got to stop this! But then, Henry realizes that she's serious. "Don't you all see?"

"See what?" Apollo says.

"*Parad!* We looked, we listened."

Apollo and Jo might not understand, but Henry does. It's terrifying, and his stomach knots, but he knows exactly what she's saying. "The *answer*," he says. "It appeared. Vlad Luxor is giving a parade and a fair. This is a chance for Rocco to hide in plain sight. It'll be crowded. What a perfect way for Vlad Luxor to see Rocco but not notice him. *This* is what we have to do next."

"Captain Every was right all along," Pirate Girl says.

CHAPTER 20

An Invitation to the Tower

This is going to be a snap!" Apollo says. "Rocco, don't you worry. You won't be a naked lizard much longer. Hiding in plain sight when there are lots of people around is the easiest thing in the world."

Henry knows this is true. There have been many days at school, surrounded by children, when he's been sure no one's noticed him at all.

"He said the parade is today," Jo says. "We need to find out when and where."

"There are signs everywhere. We only need to follow them," Pirate Girl says. She sounds like a fortune-teller.

But Pirate Girl is right— there *are* signs everywhere,

A Fortune-Teller

posters on every pole and post and tree. Everyone is elbowing and shoving to get close enough to see.

"'Parad at noon. Fare following,'" Pirate Girl reads from the sign pasted on the nearest lamppost.

"Oh no," Apollo says. "Oh *no!*"

"What?" Jo edges in to have a look.

"'Location: Tower Grounds,'" Apollo reads. Henry's heart cinches. He puts his arms around his own thin shoulders. "The parade and fair are at *the tower.*"

"*No one* has been to the tower since Vlad Luxor moved in," Jo says, horrified. "Except the awful people who work for him."

"And spies, don't forget," Pirate Girl says.

"We can't go up there!" Apollo runs a panicked hand through his handsome hair. "It's a trap."

It seems that the rest of the villagers agree, because all at once, whispers of *It's a trap, It's a trap* begin to spread like a bad rash.

"Maybe it's not a trap at all," Pirate Girl whispers. "Vlad Luxor *does* like to celebrate himself."

"And *everyone* will be there. If there are lots and lots of people, we'll have safety in numbers," Henry says. Honestly, even to himself, this sounds as doubtful as one of the ads in the back of *Amazing Stories* magazine.

"Are you kidding?" Apollo says. "Who would be foolish enough to go? Up there, you wouldn't have a chance! Down here, you could at least run or hide."

One of the Ads in the Back of
Amazing Stories *Magazine*

"They *have* to go! He told them to." It's hard for Henry to imagine defying *anyone* more powerful.

"This is what you call a no-win situation. A double bind. A catch-22, which means a dilemma from which there is no escape, because of—"

"We get it, Apollo." Pirate Girl's voice is testy. This avalanche of knowledge right now is only making Henry more anxious, too.

"The point is, you can get stuck up there forever, or at least have a chance down here."

Around them, the woman with the stroller hurries off. The people with their shopping bags disappear in all directions. The diners with their napkins still tucked into their collars seem to vanish. Ms. Esmé Silvooplay turns the sign at the French bakery from OPEN to CLOSED. Sir Loinshank Jr. of Big Meats does the same. Miss Becky, of Creamy Dreamy

Dairy, locks the door of her shop and rushes away, her apron still on.

The children are suddenly alone on the street. The only other people in sight are a few workers at the Always Open, now shut, who are scraping off the old name of the store and painting on a new one. There are three letters so far. VLA. *Vlad's.*

"Well, that settles it," Apollo says. "No one's going, so we certainly aren't. It's much too dangerous. Besides, we can't hide in plain sight if it's just us."

"That's not the attitude that will turn a naked lizard back into a little brother," Pirate Girl reminds him. "Captain Every said a plan would appear, and it has. What's more of a sign than an actual *sign*?"

"No way," Apollo says.

"We have to! It's our *duty*. Captain Every *told* us our courage would be tested," Pirate Girl says. "Think about what it was like, really *like*, for his ship to be battered to a million pieces in a storm, to swim to shore holding only a piece of planking. Imagine how terrifying it was to take part in a ritual involving a troop of orangutans and a large snake! And then, malaria! Bizarre hallucinations from jungle fever! Rivers of sweat! I know how bad and scared I felt when I had an awful earache."

"She's right," Jo says. "And I have to think about what it was like, really *like*, for Manuela Sáenz to fight in a battle on the slopes of the Pichincha volcano. Besides, Vlad

Bizarre Hallucinations from Jungle Fever

Luxor *does* love to be celebrated and admired. Maybe it's not a trap at all. Maybe it really is just a parade and a fair."

Henry swallows his own fear. "We'll just go up the mountain, watch the parade, and get Rocco to hide in plain sight of Vlad Luxor." *Just.* The word echoes and shimmers with foolishness.

Pirate Girl fishes in her pocket, removes a watch on a chain. "It's ten thirty. And it's a long way up there. We're going to have to hurry."

"This is nuts," Apollo says.

"We have *the stuff*," Henry says, though inside, his stomach is collapsing with nerves.

"Okay, okay, but I don't think I have the stuff," Apollo says.

The children look up at the tower. It looks so cold. It looks so high and far away. No one wants to make the first move. The five of them plus Button are frozen in place.

Wait. Button.

"Where's Button?" Henry asks. "Button!" he calls, panicked. "Button, come!"

"It's okay. She's way over there," Jo says.

Henry sees Button's little white-and-brown behind trotting down Main Street, heading toward the meadow and the Circle of the Y. The place where one road goes down, down to the lighthouse, and one goes up, up to that horrible tower.

"Wait for us!" Henry calls.

CHAPTER 21

The Frightening Trip Up the Mountain

In the Circle of the Y, the children drop their bikes. The two very different roads sit on either side of them like a decision.

"Ready?" Pirate Girl asks, but no one answers, because no one would ever be ready for this.

They begin to walk up that steep, rocky path. Almost immediately, the meadow disappears, and the way ahead becomes shady. On either side of them, there's the start of a forest—ferns, a few brambles, prickly blackberry bushes, the thin trunks of young evergreen trees and pines.

"It's very shady and prickly and foresty," Pirate Girl says, freeing her sleeve from a reaching blackberry branch.

"Cold, too," Jo says, zipping her thin sweatshirt.

The damp-earth smell of the woods surrounds them. It gets shadier and pricklier and more foresty with each step. The trees begin to get larger and older. Finally, up ahead,

Henry sees it—that iron wall made of bars, and in the center, the gates themselves.

"Wow," Jo says.

None of them have ever been here before. They all stare upward. The iron bars reach toward the sky, and iron vines loop between and up and around, and the wall itself disappears right into the trees. The gates are giant and steely, and a tight row of spikes marches along the top, dull and deadly. One wouldn't dare reach a hand sideways between those bars. Those iron leaves on those iron vines look razor sharp. They could slice your hand like a knife through lunchmeat.

"Those are the scariest gates I've ever seen," Jo says.

"And they're open." Apollo shudders.

It's true. Open gates—well, usually they give the joyful sense of welcome, the feeling of excitement about what waits on the other side. But these gates are more like the open doors of a cage where a dangerous animal lies in wait, even if you can't see him yet.

"Come on," Pirate Girl says, Button at her side.

Henry follows. The moment he steps through those gates, dread crawls deep into him.

"This is a bad idea. Bad, bad, bad, bad," Apollo says.

"Bad, bad, bad, bad," Rocco squeaks.

"You're not helping, Poll," Pirate Girl says. She makes a face to remind him of the scared little brother in his pocket. "Try to hold it together. Let's focus and stay quiet."

On the other side now, the road climbs, and the sun vanishes, and the trees that border the path get taller and taller with each step, and the brush gets thicker. Under his shoes, as they trudge upward, Henry swears that the rocks feel rockier. He suddenly gets that unsettling feeling that they are mere mortals propelling through a large and dangerous universe.

Mere Mortals Propelling Through a Large and Dangerous Universe

Soon, the hike becomes so steep that walking takes real effort. Apollo's backpack begins to slouch from the weight, like a backpack with bad posture. Pirate Girl's cheeks are red, and she's puffing hard. Even Button's pace slows. Henry feels his muscles pull, and there's a burn in his chest.

No one says another word. Rocco falls asleep, cradled and swayed by the ride in Apollo's pocket. The only sound is the *crunch-crunch, crunch-crunch* of their footsteps against rock, set in the eerie silence of bad stuff about to happen.

Henry looks up. The evergreens and pines are immense and ancient, and their boughs reach out like the arms of giants. In that forest . . . Well, who knows? Who can tell? Anything might be in there. It looks dark and deep enough to get lost in forever.

Henry shivers. The fur on Button's back is up. Pirate Girl walks beside him.

Up ahead, he sees Jo take Apollo's hand. This seems the wrong order of things. Henry shouldn't be back here with the girl who has stuffed pockets and leather boots. He should be up there, with the girl who has the brown eyes and shiny hair, but this is no time for romantic troubles.

Now Henry can also hear the sorts of rustles and cracks and snaps that you always hear in the woods. The kind that make shudders sneak up the back of your neck. Oh, it's creepy.

"Wait," Pirate Girl says. "What's that?"

"What's what?" Apollo says.

They stop, standing as still as possible to listen.

"That."

It's the sound of thunder moving in, but it isn't thunder. It's the rumble of tires and the growl of an engine heading up the mountain. And laughter, getting closer.

It's a truck. *Trucks.*

The children hunch together at the side of the road. Dust kicks up as the first truck rolls and roars by, carrying the strange and huge insect-like contraptions of fair rides. And then another passes, packed with machinery and signs. Henry spots two of them: GIANT CORNDOGS, one reads. SLUSHY YUMEES, reads another. When he was little, the good workers from Everything Storage set up the parade and fair in town. Now the trucks say Everything Vlad's, and the fair is on this

Scary Face with Mutton-Chop Sideburns

mountain, and the drivers of the trucks are tower people who have scary faces with mutton-chop sideburns.

"At least we know there's really going to be a fair," Jo says.

"I told you. He likes to celebrate himself," Pirate Girl says.

They keep walking. It seems like they've been on that road forever. "This is the longest, tallest mountain in the world," Apollo pants.

That's how it feels, anyway, even if they all know that the longest, tallest mountain is really somewhere in the Jaggeds. Still, the children are dragging their feet and growing quite weary. Now that they've gotten higher, Henry can see huge, nerve-racking drops where the cliff face plunges all the way down to the ground. In other spots, Henry can hear trickles of water, as if there's a cool, thirst-quenching stream somewhere inside those woods. But more than anything, they see the tower growing larger and larger as they get closer. It is so, so much more colossal than it seems from below. Fifty-eight stories, but fifty-eight *immense* stories.

Finally, Jo says, "Am I seeing what I think I'm seeing?" They stop. Pirate Girl wipes the sweat from her forehead. Henry's face is shiny from heat and sweat, too. Jo has her hoodie tied around her waist.

"Holy stromboli. A wall," Pirate Girl says, but her words are filled with awe.

"Is that *gold*?" Apollo asks.

When Best Farriver was their RM, anyone could ride up the mountain road, and once you were at the top, you were in a wide, open space, with a small village and a little town square and grassy park in front of the old stone tower. But now, in addition to the horrible iron barrier on the bottom of the mountain, there is this wall at the top, circling the tower and whatever else is inside.

But it's an astonishing wall, they can tell as they get closer—beautiful and shimmery. It's so bright and gleaming, it's almost hard to look at. Apollo puts a hand over his eyes to see better. He steps toward it slowly. The children and Button follow, and Rocco is awake now, too, his tiny lizard head twitching left and right at the sight. Even Button seems mesmerized. The gold wall *is* beautiful, and it *is* impressive, and even Henry wants to run his hand along it, because evil things can compel you and stir you and draw you forward.

"I wonder if it's real," Apollo says. "I wish I had a magnet, and then I could test it. A magnet doesn't stick to gold."

"Just a sec." Pirate Girl reaches into one pocket and hands over a U-shaped bar.

Apollo holds it to the wall, and draws it away again. "It's real."

"Never mind the wall," Jo says. "Look at the *tower*."

Henry looks beyond the wall and up. This close, that tower is enormous. The black mirrors of it rise until he can barely see the top. They glisten and reflect the gold, promising treasure and more treasure everywhere you look. He blinks and blinks. It's very hard not to feel captivated by it all.

Pirate Girl claps her hands. "Snap out of it, people! Never mind all the shiny stuff. Remember why we're here. Check it out." She hooks her thumb toward the gates a few steps away. *These* gates are gilded, intricate and radiant. And they're open, too, same as the frightening iron ones at the bottom of the mountain.

"Another wall, another gate," Henry sighs.

"Look at the banner up there," Apollo says. It's blue and gold with satiny fringe, stretching from end to end across the top of the entrance.

FAYRE, it reads.

Pirate Girl snickers. She makes that terrible *ckkk* sound in her throat again.

No one dares to cross the threshold yet. Jo tries to peer inside from where she stands, rising on her toes, craning her neck. "It's hard to see, but there's a fair for sure."

"It seems very quiet for a celebration," Henry says.

"Too quiet," Apollo says.

They stand in a huddle at the entrance. Henry's scared to cross to the other side, but he feels slow and confused, too, as if he's under a strange spell. The gold is just so dazzling.

His heart pounds, *ba-bamp, ba-bamp,* as if to keep reminding him who he truly is.

Henry shakes himself from the glint and enchantment. Or maybe that's Pirate Girl, shaking his arm.

"Come on, guys. Ready? Let's go turn a lizard back into a boy," she says.

CHAPTER 22

Rocco's Moment Arrives

And strangely, this time they *are* ready, the way you're ready when you've waited and worried for a terrible thing for so long that finally, *finally*, the waiting seems worse than the terrible thing itself. As they step through that gate and under the banner, Henry's surprised to see that they're in the same little village that was there when Best Farriver was their RM. He had no idea what they might find, but a familiar town square stretches in front of them, with shops and little thin houses on either side, and beyond that, the grassy park, which sits in front of the tower. Now, though, Vlad's workers live in the village's tall thin houses, and the shops all seem to sell a variety of objects featuring images of Vlad Luxor, and many rides and games are going up in the grassy park, and the tower is a gleaming pillar of black.

Way up ahead, on the left side of the park, Henry sees the Swing Zing and the Loop de Loop and the Tummy Twirl and the Cage Lurch. The scary men with the mutton-chop sideburns wrench and screw bolts into place, and then hurriedly take their tools to the next rickety display.

On the right, Henry spots booths of food. Dino Toes, Banana Sticks, Rainbow Bloops, and more. Tower workers seem to be frying and freezing and dipping things into Candied Dashes and Dots. There are games over there, as well—the Ring Bottle Toss, the Water Zapper, the Clown Mouth Chuck, the Rodent Blammer. But no one else is on the street.

"It's so . . . still," Jo says.

It's the kind of still that makes you hold your breath. And it's eerie, how chilly Henry feels even in the heat of summer.

"We're the only ones here, except for those few workers," Apollo says.

"No," Pirate Girl whispers, turning pale. "No, we're not."

Henry follows Pirate Girl's gaze, through the entire village, past the displays on the grass to the tower itself.

He sees him now, too.

Vlad Luxor.

Vlad Luxor, one of the most evil HRMs in history, exiting the tower doors, taking the steps to the grass. He strolls the cleared path that runs through the middle of the fair, veering right and left to greet every single person present. He interrupts the work of the scary men, who rise to their feet when he approaches. He pumps their hands, and thumps them on the back, and smiles a big smile. Then he heads to the food booths to do the same with the workers peeling bananas and dunking Bloops into frosting.

"I've never seen him this close before," Jo says.

"Me neither," Henry says, his voice quivering like violin strings.

They can hear him, too, even at that distance. "Welcome!" Vlad Luxor booms. "Greetings!"

"He's coming this way, I know it," Apollo whispers.

"I think the fair really *is* to celebrate him," Jo says. She puts her thin sweatshirt on again, and zips it all the way to her neck. She hides her hands up the sleeves.

Now he reaches the far end of the town square. "So glad I could come! So nice to meet me!" Vlad Luxor shouts. He waves toward the shops to his right. He waves toward the shops to his left.

"Who is he waving at? There's no one here," Jo whispers.

"His reflection, I think," Pirate Girl says. Her eyes glitter with giggles, but then she blinks and is serious again.

"Find your spot for the parade so you can get a great view of me!" he shouts.

"He's heading over," Apollo says. "I told you he would!"

"Rocco! Do you think you can try to hide in plain sight? All you have to do is be seen but not noticed. Just stick your head out of Apollo's pocket!" Pirate Girl says.

"I doubt there will be any hiding in plain sight," Jo says. "He's staring right at us."

It's true. Vlad is veering straight toward them with his

hand out. Rocco ducks down into Apollo's pocket with a tiny squeal, and who could blame him. The children step out of the street and flatten themselves as far against Vlad's Gift Shop as they can get. Even with Henry's eyes squinched half shut, he can see the figurines of Vlad in the window, and the dishes and mugs featuring Vlad's face. In the bookshop right next door, he can read the titles of the books that all have Vlad's photo on the cover: *The Glory of Me. The Art of Me. My Power: The Story of Vlad Luxor.*

Henry's knees begin to knock together, and any readiness he or the other children felt as they walked under that banner vanishes same as your shadow when a cloud crosses the sun. Henry sticks his hand in his pocket to feel for his lucky marble. He's never needed luck more than now.

"Oh no, oh no, here he comes," Jo cries softly. Pirate Girl shoves her hands into her armpits so she won't have to shake his hand. Button whimpers, and Rocco isn't hiding in plain sight, he's just plain hiding. Apollo is too frozen to move.

"Nice to see me!" Vlad Luxor booms.

"I don't want to do this anymore," Apollo says.

"Me neither," Jo says.

"Wanna go home," Rocco peeps from inside Apollo's pocket.

If you remember being afraid, very afraid, take that feeling and multiply it by the biggest number you can think of. Henry is trying hard, hard, hard to remember why he's there. He's reminding himself about goodness and love and little brothers and kind mothers. About friendship, and doing the right thing, and being brave, like his grandfather said. He's trying to remember all his strengths: how he can swim a crawl stroke, and find the North Star, and identify cloud formations—cumulus versus stratus versus cumulonimbus.

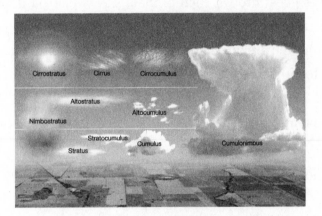

Cumulus Versus Stratus Versus Cumulonimbus

"We never should have come," Apollo says, as quietly as a person can speak.

"Let's get out of here," Jo says. "Now."

Right then, though, and so very suddenly, too, a squirrel drops from the rooftop and lands on the sidewalk. Jo screams. Needleman, with his envelope-thin body and pointed nose, appears out of nowhere and shoves Henry between the shoulder blades, into the street.

It happens so fast that Henry doesn't even have a moment to feel shock. All at once, Vlad is grasping Henry's hand in his. Vlad Luxor's skin feels chilly and plump and damp, and he has thick fingers and a swallowing palm. As Vlad's flesh touches Henry's, it's as if Henry can feel his spine shriveling and his blood stopping in his veins. He snatches his hand back, and then he sees Needleman forcing Pirate Girl's hand into Vlad Luxor's, and then Apollo's, and then Jo's, and a shiver goes through each of them. Every hair on Button's back is standing up in a straight line.

"And who are these happy little people?" Vlad Luxor asks. His breath smells like canned soup. His teeth are the color of an old pair of dice. His eyes don't even look human. They are pointed and sharp, like two darts heading straight for a target.

Two Darts Heading Straight for a Target

"Who are they?" Needleman says. "Just your average children. No one special." He lowers his brows in a threatening fashion. "Young people, say thank you for this wonderful day of joy and fun."

"Thank you for this wonderful day of joy and fun," the children say.

"Your pleasure!" Vlad Luxor says. "Needleman! What's next on the schedule? Where am I supposed to go now that I've greeted my fans?"

"To the head of the parade, behind those buildings, where the floats are lining up. It will be my honor to show you." Needleman glares at the children, and the look jabs Henry like a knife. "The parade will be starting any minute, little ones. Now go find your spot! You'll have to hurry, since it's getting crowded. Oh, look! There's a free area. How lucky to find a patch among the throngs! Quickly." Needleman grabs a handful of Henry's skin under his arm and squeezes. Henry's so thin that he feels this pinch right through his bones. And then Needleman's icy breath shoots through his ear. "If any of you move, you'll be sorry. Come, Mr. Reese!" he says to the squirrel.

Needleman takes Vlad Luxor's elbow and guides him across the square. The children watch until the two men and one squirrel completely disappear.

"I feel sick," Apollo says.

Do you know that feeling when you've touched something extremely unpleasant—a scratchy fabric, a sticky goo, or maybe a dead who-knows-what that you accidentally picked up? This is what Henry's experiencing now, after shaking Vlad Luxor's hand. He wipes his hand on his shorts, trying to make the feeling go away.

"Gross," Pirate Girl says, and does the same.

Apollo gazes down at his palm as if he's expecting to

see his skin change to the rippled texture of a crocodile.

"Ugh." Jo shakes her fingers. "We need to get out of here. This is too awful to stand."

"He told us not to move!" Apollo says.

"We can't *leave!*" Pirate Girl says. "And not because of Needleman! Have we all forgotten why we're here? A *real* chance for Rocco to hide in plain sight, in all the commotion and crowd of a parade!" Pirate Girl looks around the empty town square. There's not a soul around. "Well. Maybe it's still early." She fetches her watch from the pocket of her pants, and then sighs. "Eleven fifty-eight."

In the distance, the rides creak and sway. Smoke and smells of frying things drift their way from the food stalls. Henry spots a sign for foot-long corndogs. A ray of light hits it, a good ray, an important ray, the kind you see shooting from the sky every now and then. It seems like a signal, maybe from a faraway beam, a lighthouse beam. A ray of encouragement to go on.

*A Ray of Light
on a Corndog Sign*

Henry gives himself a silent pep talk. It's about being all he can be and climbing the highest

mountains and getting up when you're knocked down—
the stuff you hear in ads for athletic shoes.

"We have to at least try," he tells everyone else. "Come out
of there, Rocco."

"Uh-uh," comes the tiniest lizard voice from Apollo's
pocket.

"I understand why you hid when Vlad Luxor came," Henry
pleads. "I wanted to hide, too. But you can't hide in plain
sight without being *in plain sight*. Please come out. This
could be your *moment.*"

"Henry's right, Rocco. We have to try." Apollo reaches
into his pocket and grabs Rocco. And, yes, a lizard's eyes
are already round and bulgy, but Rocco's eyes are even
rounder and bulgier now from terror. "This is our chance.
You can sit here on my shoulder. I'll be right underneath
you the whole time."

"Please, Rocco," Henry says gently. "*Please* just stay where
Vlad Luxor can look your way but not see you. You can become a boy again! And then we can figure out how to get
out of here."

In spite of his brave words, Henry is nervous, very nervous. Because, well, look. The children are sticking out like
a bunch of zebras in a savannah full of lions.

"Eleven fifty-nine," Pirate Girl reports.

"We're all alone," Apollo says. He looks scared out of his
wits.

"Not exactly," Pirate Girl says. Needleman is hurrying

across the square. His hands are set in small fists at his sides, and his grin gleams as sharp as those awful tools the dentist uses on your teeth.

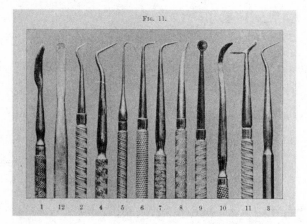

Those Awful Tools the Dentist Uses on Your Teeth

"Lovely day for a parade, isn't it, children?" He settles beside them. Mr. Reese, the squirrel, sits at his heels. "It's a good thing you came, because Vlad Luxor wants to see happy children at his parade, and now you will be *happy children at his parade.*"

A whistle blows. No, it *shrieks*, like the brakes of a train. The sound whips right through Henry's ears and pierces their drums. It is shatteringly loud. But no one even dares to flinch.

It's twelve o'clock.

CHAPTER 23

A Most Awful Parade

Before they see anything, they hear it: music. Trumpets and cymbals, clarinets and tubas, a big drum. The uproar causes poor Button's ears to twitch in pain. Ladies wearing little sequined shorts and tiny bikini tops come down the street, twirling batons.

Pirate Girl looks at Jo and rolls her eyes.

Jo rolls her eyes back in agreement.

"Puh-leaze," Pirate Girl says, much too loudly.

Henry doesn't know where to look. It's all quite embarrassing. Now, though, behind the sequin-clad ladies come two young men carrying a large banner. Henry has never seen any of these people before, either. They *all* must work in the tower. The banner features a large image of Vlad Luxor. It's just his head and shoulders, and one waving arm. Vlad for the People, the banner reads.

"Applaud," Needleman commands.

The children clap. The parade route—through town,

down the cleared path through the grassy park and to the tower—is entirely empty except for them.

A large float rolls by. It features an enormous banana made out of crepe paper. Go Bananas for Vlad, the float reads. Courtesy of Vlad's Grocery.

Apollo edges his foot over and nudges Henry's, and Henry nudges back. The Always Open is gone for sure, and here's the proof. It's *another* one of the things they most love, ruined. What next? Destroying the endangered animals of the planet? Blowing up the planet itself? Henry's insides roil with both fear and anger.

Now an elephant wearing a satin cape lumbers down the street. A lady sits on top in a matching satin outfit. She is waving and blowing kisses to the crowd that is made up of four children, one dog, one naked lizard, one evil man, and one hideous squirrel. Henry thinks this is the same woman who was dunking Bloops into frosting.

"An elephant," Apollo says.

"Animals are not entertainme—" Pirate Girl says, and Henry jabs his elbow into her side. If Needleman hears, all he has to do is speak one word of this to Vlad Luxor, and he'll turn *her* into an elephant.

"Ow," she says.

Henry makes his eyes big and tightens his jaw to say STOP IT without actually saying STOP IT.

"Don't tell me what to do," she snaps.

Henry wonders if Grandfather was wrong about the DNA

154

and *the stuff* and about them being the *right children*, because they are clearly the most wrong right children anyone could find.

"Wave to the nice lady," Needleman commands.

They wave.

"Harder. And with more enthusiasm," he says.

Henry waves like he's lost at sea and hopes to be spotted by the rescue plane. A float of a giant rooster comes next. COCK-A-DOODLE-DOO FOR VLAD! the sign reads. The rooster has giant blue eyes and a beak large enough to chomp you to bits.

When they see the final float roll forward, though, the children gasp. Not a gasp of mere shock, but one of outright horror. The float features a large jail made out of plaster and paint. Inside, there's a

A Beak Large Enough to Chomp You to Bits

yellow-beaked starling, sitting on a perch. They know who this is. It's their poor school librarian, Mrs. Trembly.

"Caw, caw, caw!" Mrs. Trembly says.

OBEY THE LAW, the float reads, in letters made out of red crepe paper roses.

Now the parade is almost over. A group of trumpeters marches forward. Their trumpets are decorated with dropped swaths of velvet, and they're wearing uniforms of blue and gold satin. They stop in front of the children and play a herald for the arrival of a king.

And here he comes—Vlad Luxor, riding very high up on an elaborately decorated stretcher. It's as wide as a mattress and is carried by the scary men with the mutton-chop side-burns, looking uncomfortable now in their satin uniforms. Atop Vlad Luxor's ice-cream-swirl hair sits a gold crown. Sweat rolls from his face, which ladies in sequins dab at with handkerchiefs. He *must* be hot. Over his gold and blue satin suit, he wears an ermine cloak, favored by kings of the past.

It's time. It's finally their chance for Rocco to hide in plain sight. The children meet one another's eyes. Henry feels Pirate Girl's hand slip into his, and Jo is holding her other one, and Apollo holds hers. Henry can feel the weight of Button leaning against his legs. He glances at Rocco, and if you've ever seen a reptile tremble, well, that's what's happening now.

An Ermine Cloak, Favored by Kings of the Past

Rocco is shaking, and his big orbs blink and blink. Henry holds his breath. He silently pleads to Rocco. *Please, Rocco,* he thinks. *Please don't dive into Apollo's pocket. Don't hide or make a move. Don't be silly. Don't do anything to get attention.*

PLEASE.

Vlad Luxor smiles. His chin is raised, and his face is tilted to the sky to take in every admiration. He waves to one side, and then he waves to the other, even though no one is there. And it would be ridiculous, you would laugh your silly head off, if he weren't so cruel and evil and dark. If he weren't so *dangerous.*

Henry feels a horrible twist in his stomach. He could be sick. Pirate Girl squeezes his hand. Apollo lets out a little groan. Henry sneaks another look at Rocco, who is utterly still and utterly silent.

"Applaud," Needleman says.

They release hands and clap.

"Cheer."

They cheer.

"Call his name, and wave your arms."

"Vlad," they say.

"Louder."

"VLAD!" they yell.

So of course, he looks over to them, to this small group of children, plus one dog and one lizard who is being absolutely one-hundred-percent perfectly well behaved. But they are the only people there, and so Vlad Luxor sets his gaze on each of them, one at a time. First he looks at Henry. When he does, Henry feels the evil of today and the evil of a million years ago. His insides turn to ice, as if he is standing right next to the coldest planet.

Standing Right Next to the Coldest Planet

Next, Vlad Luxor locks eyes with Pirate Girl, and then Jo, and then Apollo, and they each shiver in turn. And finally, it happens. Vlad Luxor stares right at Rocco, little Rocco who is doing his absolute best, better than they ever could have asked for, better than they ever could have hoped. A best that is still not good enough, because *all* of them are there in plain sight. Vlad looks at Rocco, sees him, and smiles with his yellow-white teeth.

They walked through those iron gates. They climbed the mountain. They passed underneath that banner, and stood before the most evil man on earth. They even shook his hand. They looked and listened and were aware and brave. *So* brave.

But they have failed.

CHAPTER 24
Things Get Worse

And then . . .

Things get worse. Things get way, way worse. The kind of worse where all your most terrible fears begin to come true. The parade disappears up through the park and around the tower. From behind, the children can see a long tail of toilet paper trailing from the back of Vlad Luxor's blue satin trousers. But it's not even funny. Nothing is. Henry feels empty and shivery and afraid. And their failure hits, too, with a great clap of disappointment.

"That went well," Needleman says. Mr. Reese *chee chee chees*. In squirrel language, Henry's sure this means something awful. Something like *I am about to leap on your head and scurry around in your hair.*

The children stare down at their feet. Jo takes Apollo's hand. For Henry, this is one more thing that makes the world seem as if it's lost its last hope.

"Don't you think, children? Wasn't that a stunning display?

Come on, what's with the long faces? What could you possibly be sad about? Your days are full of Lolly Sweets and dollies and trucks and rainbows. All you have to do is play and laugh and have cheerful thoughts, since children never have worries. And who is this? Why did I not notice this little slimy, disgusting reptile before?"

He looks right smack at Rocco. And Rocco—well, he continues to do an excellent job. He's not saying a word. He's being polite and quiet and unwiggly. He's the best little lizard-boy ever. Of course, he's too terrified to do anything but blink and tremble and clutch his brother's shirt with his reptile toes, but still. On top of everything else, Mr. Reese is eyeing him as if he's an especially tasty squirrel snack. It's clear, quite clear, that there will be no hiding in plain sight, not from Vlad, or Needleman, or Mr. Reese. Not from anyone.

"This is my pet lizard," Apollo says.

"He's naked."

"Yes. He's a naked lizard. *Lizardo Nakedismo*," Apollo says. "One of five thousand six hundred species of—"

"I do believe he looks a little *familiar*. I do believe he looks like a little *boy*."

Needleman winks. The wink isn't really a wink. It's a thing that's pretending to be friendly when it's not. There is nothing worse than when someone pretends to be friendly or honest or trustworthy or good or caring when they're none of those things. It's the meanest kind of trick. Henry hates him. Henry is not the hating sort, but he does. He hates Needleman with everything he has.

"I think we need to be going now," Henry says.

"Go? You just got here. Of course you won't be *going*. Don't be silly. Vlad Luxor wants all the children of the province to enjoy the fair that he has created, so you—the only children foolish enough to appear—will stay here and do as Vlad Luxor wishes."

"My parents are expecting us home," Apollo says.

"With the milk you never got, I suppose," Needleman says. "And what about your parents, Henry Every? I imagine they're checking their watches, counting the seconds until they can see their darling boy again."

When Needleman says this, Henry feels like he's a boxer who's just received a terrible blow to the head.

A Boxer Who's Just Received
a Terrible Blow to the Head

"You think I don't know who you are? Or should I say, *what* you are? I knew about you from the first time I saw you all together. Separately, you appeared to be normal, annoying, little drooling babies, but gathered in a huddle and having a *meeting* . . . Four *particular* children from four *particular* family lines . . ." He hisses the words that come next, and they sound terrible, but powerful, too. *"Spell breakers."*

The chills slither up the back of Henry's spine. The children look at each other again with horror-filled eyes that speak one truth: If Needleman knows, it won't be long until Vlad Luxor does, too.

"You're lucky that Vlad Luxor wants to see happy children at the fair," Needleman says, "or I would have gotten rid of you already. So be HAPPY. CHILDREN. AT. THE. FAIR. For now."

With one hand, Needleman grabs Henry's wrist. With the other, he reaches for Pirate Girl.

Henry tries to twist free. Pirate Girl flings one boot out and kicks him hard in the shin, but Needleman only chuckles. Henry knows it's a chuckle that isn't a chuckle, like it was a wink that wasn't a wink and a flick that was really a punch.

"Little spitfire, eh?"

Pirate Girl glares.

"You would be pretty if you weren't so ugly," he says.

"You will be eternally ugly," she says.

"What she means is—" Jo interrupts.

"What she means is that your heartless heart is as ugly as an armpit," Pirate Girl says. "With apologies to armpits."

Needleman bends down and stares straight into Pirate Girl's eyes. "I would be rid of you like *that*, small pirate," he says, snapping his fingers. "But since our magnificent and respected HRM wants to see the little children of his province having a beautiful time at a celebration in his honor, you are going to play some games. You are going to go on a ride. You, all of you, will laugh and sing and smile before you disappear forever. I hope I'm making myself clear. Am I making myself clear?"

"Very clear," Apollo says.

"Say, 'We can't wait.'"

"We can't wait," Jo says, through her gritted teeth.

"Count your blessings that I need you, you shin-kicking brats. But when I no longer do . . ." He points to Henry and Apollo and Pirate Girl and Jo and Rocco. "Gone, gone, gone, gone, gone." Finally, he points to Button. "And gone." A low growl starts in Button's throat. "For now, I am being a kind and generous man. Say, 'Thank you, Mr. Needleman.'"

"Thank you, Mr. Needleman," they say.

Needleman is squeezing Henry so tightly under the arm that his skin throbs. Needleman has Pirate Girl's arm, too, gripping her hard enough that her boots are almost up off the ground. Needleman shoves them forward. Apollo and Jo are too scared to do anything but follow. "Come along, Mr. Reese, let's take the children to a nice game."

13. Mollberg's dive.

Olympic Diver

Button eyes that squirrel and bares her teeth. *"Chee chee chee,"* Mr. Reese says. He twitches his tail. He scurries in a zigzag fashion that makes Rocco fly into Apollo's pocket like an Olympic diver.

"And don't forget to laugh and be delighted like the happy-go-lucky children you are," Needleman snarls.

CHAPTER 25

A Large Vlad Head and Other Catastrophes

Around them, Henry hears the shuffle of their own footsteps, and the creak and groan of the rides. No flies dare buzz, and no mosquitoes bite. Even the litter seems to have scurried off to hide in the sewer grates. Vlad Luxor, in his blue satin, strolls among the booths while the people from the tower eat Banana Sticks and ride the Swing Zing and play the games, still wearing their sequins and uniforms.

"I knew we shouldn't have come," Apollo whispers to Jo. Over his shoulder, Henry sees Jo take Apollo's hand again, and entwine her fingers tightly with his. Button growls even more fiercely as Mr. Reese, the squirrel,

Creepy Squirrel Claws

scurries around her legs, rubbing his creepy squirrel claws together.

"Play," Needleman commands, and the children spray shoots of water into the mouths of clowns.

"Toss," Needleman commands, and the children throw balls into tilted hoops.

"Aim," Needleman commands, and the children try to hurl darts at a wall of balloons that cannot be popped.

"Fling," Needleman commands.

They stand before a large table of milk bottles. Needleman hands them colored rings, which are supposed to land around the bottle necks. Above the booth, in every size, there are stuffed heads resembling Vlad Luxor. Pirate Girl flings her ring and misses on purpose, and so does Jo, and then Apollo. It's Henry's turn.

"Win one of the toys, child," Needleman says through his teeth. "Do you hear me?" Henry flings the ring wildly, and it hits the ground. Needleman thrusts another over the neck of the nearest bottle. "Hurrah! A winner!" he shouts, loud enough so that Vlad Luxor, eating a Crow Crunch on a stick, looks their way and beams.

Needleman shoves an enormous stuffed Vlad Luxor head at Henry. It's so huge, he can barely get his arms around it. The ice cream hair alone is almost as tall as a moderate sand dune.

Henry must hold the horrible thing next to his whole body in order to carry it. Vlad's stuffed pink face is

A Moderate Sand Dune

scratchy and hard and hideous next to Henry's innocent cheek. He has the urge to bite it, but he knows that teeth and fuzz are a shuddery mix.

Henry wonders how long they have left. The minute the fair is over, Needleman will tell Vlad about their spell-breaking abilities, and who knows what will happen then. They've got to figure out a way out of here.

"We've got to figure out a way out of here," Pirate Girl whispers, reading Henry's mind. Needleman is up ahead, clapping his hands for them to hurry along.

"We'll look and listen, and the answer will appear," Henry whispers back, though honestly, he's not so sure.

"And then we'll take the next chance we can to escape," she says.

"Ah, yes. Here we are at last," Needleman says when they catch up. "Our final stop."

Oh, horror of horrors. In front of them is the Cage Lurch,

the most rickety-looking and to-the-sky-high ride of all. It's an oblong string of cages, which rotate in a circle and rock back and forth like little midair—

Jails, Henry suddenly realizes.

The ride stops. One of the cages sits at the platform. Needleman opens the door and grins. "A perfect place to keep you until this silly fair is finished."

"Just tell us," Jo moans. "When will Vlad Luxor know about us? In two minutes or five? And what will he turn us into? Lemurs? Kitchen appliances? Nightstands? A terrible snow globe?"

A Terrible Snow Globe

"Never, and nothing, I hope, to answer your questions in order."

"What do you mean?" Apollo says. "If *you* know we're—" He doesn't even dare say the words. "Won't you tell him the first chance you get?"

"Don't be ridiculous. I can't tell him *that!* If Vlad Luxor finds out that *spell breakers* even exist, do you know what he'd do to me?

I'd be turned into a terrible snow globe! *No one* can know! It is my job to make sure there are never, ever any of you, and we've all seen what happens to people who *don't do their jobs*." Needleman stares at Mr. Reese, who twitches his tail. Then he turns to Henry. "I'd have gotten rid of your grandfather, too, but the entire province protects him, and that librarian of his knows jujitsu! Thankfully, Vlad Luxor believes he's just a harmless old lighthouse keeper. But you four . . ."

"So *you're* in danger if he finds out about us," Apollo says.

"Well, he'll never find out about you now, will he? Get in," Needleman commands.

It feels like Henry's heart has stopped, because this is what he sees: The doorway of the cage, gaping. Jo trembling. And Needleman's long, bony fingers, reaching toward Apollo, closing around the back of his neck.

CHAPTER 26

The Cage Lurch

With all due respect, sir, I wouldn't get in that thing if you paid me a million bu—" Apollo says as Needleman shoves him from behind and he lands on the little cage bench.

"Next," Needleman says.

"You are going to regret this, I promise you tha—" Jo lands hard next to Apollo. The cage swings.

Needleman scoops up Button, who snaps and twists before getting tossed inside.

"Not on your life," Pirate Girl says. She spins and kicks. "YA!"

"Ow! You little *beast*." Needleman tries to grab her.

In an incredible display of pirate ability, Pirate Girl wrenches free, grabs something from her pocket, and lunges. It's a folding pirate saber with a jeweled handle, both useful and beautiful. She spins, kicks, and thrusts. She seems to know all the moves.

"You violent thug!" Needleman yells. "Give me that,"

All the Moves

he barks to Henry, and snatches the huge stuffed head of Vlad Luxor, which he uses as a shield.

"Ughph," Pirate Girl grunts as she lunges. The tip of the saber pricks the Vlad head, and a bit of stuffing pours out.

Needleman uses the head to shove her, and Pirate Girl is forced backward. Henry tries to kick him in the rear end.

"Blrghh," Pirate Girl says, and lunges again, managing to slice off a bit of stuffed Vlad's ear.

"Now he looks like Vincent van Gogh," Apollo says. "The nineteenth-century painter who cut off his ear in a fit of—"

"Never mind that now!" Jo says. "We've got to help her!"

But it's too late for that. In a flurry of movement, Needleman shoves the Vlad head hard at Pirate Girl. She drops her saber, which clatters to the ground. Now he whirls and grabs Henry. He tosses both children into the cage, one after the other. He tries to fit the Vlad head in with them, without success. He locks their cage and presses the big button to make the ride go forward. They inch upward.

Vincent van Gogh,
the Nineteenth-Century Painter

Needleman shoves the big Vlad head, minus one ear, into the cage behind them, and then he starts the ride again.

"Chee chee chee," Mr. Reese says from below.

Their cage rises and then stops, swinging in midair. Rises, stops. Rises, stops. The children reach for each other's hands. "Oh," Jo says. "Oh, oh." It's a quiet cry of despair. No one else can even speak. Henry's voice is gone. His thin shoulders tremble. The cage rocks back and forth.

Swing-swing. Swing-swing.

Henry could be sick. Button is whimpering. They're high up now. So high that the tower grounds and the fair and even the trees get smaller and smaller below them. Next to the ride, the tower itself is black and gleaming, looking like the worst kind of forever.

"Say, 'Thank you for this wonderful day of joy and fun,'" Needleman shouts upward.

"Never!" Pirate Girl shouts back, and then spits down at him. The globber of sputum falls like a clump of half-chewed banana and lands on his shoulder.

Up, stop. Up, stop.

Swing-swing. Swing-swing. Henry's tummy swirls.

"Don't look over your shoulder," Jo says, which of course makes everyone look over their shoulder. The Vlad head above entirely fills up its own cage. Vlad's glued-on eyes look right at them.

"What are we going to do?" Jo says. They're still gripping hands, which are getting sweatier and sweatier. "He could keep us in here forever."

"If we're lucky! More likely, he's going to get rid of us the second Vlad is out of sight," Pirate Girl says.

"We're going to have to wait until Needleman leaves or, or . . . *something.* And then we'll escape." As Henry says this, the impossibility of it looms over him. Even if they could somehow get out of this locked jail cell on this high ride, they're on this mountain. Vlad Luxor's mountain.

Needleman stands below, laughing, his eyes fixed on the children in that awful cage. He seems to be enjoying himself, pushing the button, letting them rotate for a while, and then stopping them at the highest spot, where the cage swings and rocks.

"He doesn't look like he's going anywhere," Jo says.

"He can't stay there forever," Pirate Girl says as Needleman pushes the button to send them rotating again. Each time they pass him on the ground, Needleman gives a little wave. He cackles, as if the children are an amusing toy, before they start upward once more.

Now from inside Apollo's pocket comes a small and awful sound, like the last of the bathwater glugging down the drain.

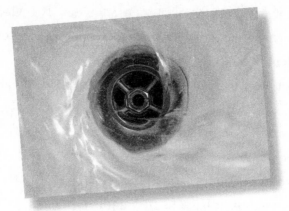

The Last of the Bathwater
Glugging Down the Drain

"Rocco?" Apollo says.

Rocco pops his head up. He's crying. No, the tiny naked lizard is sobbing. Tears roll down his itty-bitty triangle face. His reptile chest heaves up and down. His green mouth is twisted in sorrow. Henry's heart breaks. Rocco might be annoying, and his antics might have gotten them into all this trouble in the first place, but Henry remembers that he's just a little boy. If Henry is scared, he can only imagine how terrified Rocco must be.

"It's okay, buddy," Apollo says.

"We're going to get out of here," Henry says.

Henry and Apollo look at each other. It's a private look. A look that says, *The truth is, we're doomed.*

"I want my mommy," Rocco says. Henry's heart breaks double.

And then Apollo does a beautiful thing. A beautiful, brotherly thing. A thing that makes Henry remember what all of this is for: Love. And family. The kind of love and family that everyone deserves.

"I want my mommy," Apollo mimics, in spite of his own fear.

"Don't," Rocco says.

"Don't," Apollo says.

"STOP THAT RIGHT NOW, APOLLO!" Rocco says. His small lizard cheeks turn red. He makes tiny fists the size of pencil erasers.

"STOP THAT RIGHT NOW, APOLLO!" Apollo says.

Rocco punches Apollo's arm.

"Punch me again with all your might." Apollo knows that naked lizards can't do much harm. Rocco pulls back his fist and gives it all he's got. "That's the guy I know," Apollo says.

"I'm hungry," Rocco says.

"Mom gave us plenty of snacks." Apollo unzips his backpack. This is downright heroic under the circumstances. He must unclasp his hands from Henry's and Jo's. He must act normal, and give out foil packages, when absolutely no one is thinking about food except Rocco. Apollo offers everyone a slab of Choco Butter, while Button gets a Carrot Apple Bling Bar. Henry isn't sure chocolate is part of the regular diet for naked lizards, but Rocco is gobbling it up like a boy, not a reptile. Apollo and Jo and Pirate Girl unwrap the shiny paper for Rocco's sake. It's hot in there, and the sun has blazed all day, so the chocolate is a melty mess. They practically have to lick it off the wrapper. These are the *unhappiest* children eating chocolate that you've ever seen.

"Wait," Apollo says.

"What?" Henry feels a lift of hope. Apollo is the smartest of them all. He's sure to have a great idea.

"Why didn't I think of this before?"

"Tell us!" Jo says. She's thinking the same thing as Henry.

"My walkie-talkie! I have a *walkie-talkie*. All I have to do is radio for help!"

Of course Apollo has a walkie-talkie, because before today, he had everything he could ever want in the world. Apollo hunts around in his backpack. He's the smartest of them all, and he has everything a boy could want, but Henry isn't so sure about this idea. They're up on a mountain, for one. And for another—

"Who can you even radio?" Pirate Girl asks.

"Exactly." Henry sighs. There are no police officers or government officials in their town anymore. At least, none who will stand up to Vlad Luxor.

"My dad," Apollo says. "He always has his with him."

"My mother would come, too," Jo says.

It is a lovely, shining idea—parents climbing into their cars and riding up this mountain to save them from evil. Fighting off Needleman with the cleaver from the kitchen of Rio Royale or some tool from the Dante garage. But Henry doesn't believe the same things that Apollo and Jo do. Not about parents. Not about the bad that bad people are capable of.

Apollo finds his walkie-talkie. The ride creaks and groans. He's about to push the *talk* button when Pirate Girl speaks.

"Even if they could help us, *they* would be in danger then. Don't you see?"

This hadn't even occurred to Apollo. Or even to Jo. They've always lived in the cozy, safe nests of their families. Their parents have always been bigger than danger, able to make things right, no matter what. They can't even *imagine* that this might not be true. But Henry can. He can imagine *a lot* of things. He wonders if maybe Pirate Girl can, too.

The children are at the highest point of the ride again when Needleman stops it. The cage swings, back and forth, back and forth. It squeaks and wobbles like the creepy old ceiling fan that you must nervously watch.

"How about another spin on the wheel, little hamsters!" Needleman shouts. He hits the button again. The cage

The Creepy Old Ceiling Fan That You Must Nervously Watch

lurches. And right then, Apollo's walkie-talkie slips from his sticky chocolaty fingers.

He cries out, but no cry can undo the thing that is happening: the transmitter, the last link to Apollo's mom and dad, to Jo's mother, tumbling through the air like an astronaut through the atmosphere. It lands with a crack against the hard earth and, like their dream of rescue, shatters to pieces.

CHAPTER 27

Danger at Great Heights

Below them, Needleman laughs and laughs. When they pass him near the ground, he waggles a broken bit of the walkie-talkie at them. "Were you going to call your *mommies*?" He cackles.

Button begins to snarl and paw at the mesh of the cage as they rise again. Jo looks like she might cry, and this, as well as their dire situation and the zinging rush of chocolate, sends a renewed rush of resolve through Henry.

"He'll *have* to walk away for a moment. To eat, to go to the bathroom, *something*," he says.

"Plus, I have *this*." From her pocket, Pirate Girl removes a Swiss Army Safari Knife, Model 5400.

"Wow," Henry says, in awe. It's extraordinarily impressive, the top tier of pocket knives. Not only

Swiss Army Safari Knife, Model 5400

does it have a jumbo-sized blade, but it also has a saw, a screwdriver, a bottle opener, and an extra-long and sturdy corkscrew.

"It even has the hidden toothpick, which I've been very careful not to lose," Pirate Girl says.

"Can you pick this lock?" Apollo says, his eyes wide.

"Of course I can," she says. "I *think* I can. Well, who knows. I've never picked a lock before."

"Maybe you should practice," Jo says. "And then the moment Needleman steps away, you can spring us free."

"When we're close to the ground and not up here, hopefully," Apollo says.

"He *will* have to leave at some point," Jo says.

Henry swears that Jo's beautiful voice right then travels to something or someone who isn't evil, who guards goodness, who allows the right thing to happen at the right time, because even from way up there, they can suddenly hear Vlad Luxor.

"Needleman!" he booms. "Needleman, I want more photographs!"

"Photographs?"

"Lots of photographs of me and this sensational fair that I've generously given to the people! Photographs of me eating a giant corndog. Me winning prizes. Me and the laughing, happy children!"

"Now?"

"Of course now! Where is your camera?"

"Camera?"

"You don't have a camera? You know that I always need a camera. Snapshots, images, videos! Me looking to the left. Me looking to the right. Me looking serious. Me looking amused."

"Of course!" Needleman recovers. "Of course I have a camera. Let me get it. Right away!"

"And what is wrong with that ride, Needleman? It keeps starting and stopping. I love when the little baskets spin around."

"Nothing is wrong with the ride, sir! It's working perfectly!"

Needleman hits the button of the Cage Lurch, which begins its slow rotation, this time without stopping. He sends the children a warning glare before trotting toward the tower.

"We don't have time to practice after all," Henry says.

There's no need to tell Pirate Girl this. She's already on her knees, working the toothpick into the lock.

"I can't . . . I don't know . . ." Her face is knotted in concentration, sweaty from stress and the heat of their bodies in that cage. There's barely room for her to move her elbows, with all of them and Button squished inside.

"Hurry!" Apollo says. "We're getting close to the ground."

"It's harder than you think. I can't feel anything in there." Pirate Girl wiggles the toothpick.

"Is there some little latch or something?" Jo asks.

"I don't know! I'm doing the best I can!"

"He's heading into the tower," Jo reports. "We only have a few minutes."

"Oh no. We're going up again," Apollo says.

"High. Very high," Rocco says.

Rocco is right. They are way, way up there. "I'm not sure we want the door to unlock right n—" Henry says, just as the cage springs free. The door pops open and sways toward the wide-open sky. Pirate Girl screams. Her hands are still on the latch. The front half of her body swings with the door as she holds on, her legs still on the metal floor but sliding fast.

"Help!" she cries.

Henry flings himself down to catch her. When he does, his lucky marble flies from his shorts, rolls across the cage floor, and drops off the edge, disappearing forever. What this says about luck and gravity—well, he can't bear to think about that right now. With one arm, he grips Pirate Girl around the middle, and with the other, he holds tight to the side of the cage. Pirate Girl's eyes are squeezed shut, and Henry can't bear to look either. It is so, so far down. Things are falling from Pirate Girl's pockets now. A canteen flies through the air and crashes to the ground. An old can of sardines tumbles and falls.

An Old Can of Sardines

"Hang on. Please hang on!" Jo cries. Henry feels Jo's two hands grasp one of his ankles, followed by Apollo's hands gripping his other. And then, there's the nip of terrier teeth on the cuff of his shorts.

The cage swings. The joints creak like an old ship. Behind them, the giant Vlad Luxor head leers.

"No one move. Keep the cage as still as possible," Henry says. He's holding Pirate Girl with all his might, but he has the small shoulders and thin arms of a gentle boy with no meat on his bones. With every little swing, he feels Pirate Girl slip. She opens her eyes and looks at him, and he looks at her, and he sees a sight that tears him apart. Pirate Girl, the tough, challenging, and never-afraid Pirate Girl, is crying.

"Pirate Girl," he says. Henry's voice wobbles. His throat gets tight, and his own eyes water, and he wishes he could tell her the million things he already knows about feeling afraid and small and falling.

"We're going down. We're going down!" Apollo shouts.

"He's still in the tower," Jo says. "We're almost there. We're almost on the ground."

The ground, the beautiful, beloved earth, seems to rise to meet them.

"Now!" Apollo says.

"Go, Button!" Henry commands, and Button jumps, and all them, even poor Pirate Girl, tumble onto the platform.

"He's coming!" Jo cries. "Needleman's coming out of the tower!"

"Run!" Apollo yells.

CHAPTER 28
Scary Men Give Chase

The empty cage begins to rise again, the open door hanging like a loose tooth. The children race through the grassy park, past the game booths and the food, past the tower workers, who don't make a move to stop them until they see Mr. Reese zigging and zagging and leaping from tree to tree after them.

Henry has never run like this in his life. He didn't even know he *could* run like this, his breath coming in hard puffs, his thin legs pumping, fleeing as fast as a cheetah.

Apollo is in the lead. Even after all of the upset the day has brought so far (with so much more, the worst, still coming, alas), he remains quite handsome. Apollo sprints the way he does during recess, and during the times he dashes to the farthest-most corner of the baseball field to catch a fly ball.

Button races at Apollo's heels. She's a dog champion, charging at full speed. Pirate Girl bolts, too, the pirate beads in her hair flying out behind her. This time, Jo runs beside

The Farthest-Most Corner of the Baseball Field

Henry, the two of them side by side, and so Henry does maybe the bravest thing he's done the entire day, because sometimes love takes the most courage of all. He reaches for her hand. They run together, through the small town square now, down the street to the gates. It has been the worst day of his life, but for one brief moment, it's like he has wings.

They cross back under the banner. Henry's heart pounds like a tumbling boulder, and his legs cramp and knot. But then, he hears the footsteps. Back behind him, heavy boots hit the stones of the town square. Henry looks over his shoulder. Oh, it's horrible. The drivers of those trucks are coming, the men with the scary faces and the mutton-chop sideburns. They're following Mr. Reese, giving chase same as he is, coming closer and closer, too, the gap between those men and the children shrinking with each step.

They are back on that mountain road, but this small group of escaping children and one dog are easy to see. "We're in full sight! We're in full sight, Henry!" Pirate Girl yells, and she's right. They're in full sight of *everyone*, not just the men and Mr. Reese and Needleman, but Vlad himself. If he spots them running from his fair, he'll surely turn them into piles of clay or sparrows or garden statues.

There's a single, terrible place that will give them a chance to hide.

Of course, it is also a most dangerous place. Exceedingly, terribly dangerous. It's dark in there. And endless. And immense. And full of trees that whisper, and creeks that gush. The dampest gloom might swallow you up. And if you're there at night, well, good luck to you.

"The forest! Head into the forest," Henry shouts.

CHAPTER 29

Henry Uses His Skills

Immediately, the boughs of the trees wrap around the children like an enormous cloak. The sky disappears. Above them, there are only the needles of pine trees dripping dew, and on all sides, the branches of evergreens drop sticky sap onto their skin. At the children's feet, the ground is so thick with brush and ferns and prickles that they can barely move forward. Even Button is having a hard time making her way over fallen logs and through thorns and brambles. Everywhere they look, there is only forest and forest and more forest.

The way they came—it's gone. Henry wishes he had his lucky marble, but that's gone, too.

"We're going to get lost, if we're not already," Apollo says. Rocco's head sticks out of Apollo's pocket. He's looking around with his bulgy lizard eyes, and his lizard tongue flicks in and out.

"Shh," Henry says. They can still hear the voices of Vlad's men in the far-off distance. Plus, he's trying to remember all the things he knows from his *Ranger Scout Handbook*, sixth edition. *What to do if lost in a forest: Remain calm. Find shelter. Make a fire. Locate a water source.*

"I wish I had my saber," Pirate Girl says. "But I do have this."

What she pulls out of her pocket next . . . Well, it fills Henry with astonishment and gratitude and awe.

It's another watch.

But not *just* another watch—it's the Tellzall 9-in-1 Timepiece of Adventure, with a glow-in-the-dark compass, weather forecaster, signalling device, and the world's smallest ballpoint pen.

"Wow," Henry says. "That's incredible." Pirate Girl *and* her pockets—they just continue to be full of surprises. She seems to be what every Ranger Scout aspires to be: prepared for anything.

Pirate Girl holds the instrument in the flat of her hands, determining their direction. "If we want to head south, we keep going straight."

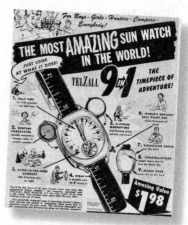

The Tellzall 9-in-1
Timepiece of Adventure

"Are you sure?" Apollo says. "I could swear we're going in circles."

"It's getting dark, too," Jo says.

"Dark," Rocco repeats.

"And cold," Jo says. She rubs her arms.

"Cold," Rocco repeats again. And not because he's being a bratty little brother, but because he's a scared and tired naked lizard.

"We go straight," Pirate Girl says. Then she checks the time. "It's just after five o'clock."

Apollo swats an insect on his neck. "We have some daylight left. The sun sets at seven ten in the northern climates this time of year."

"There is much less light, though, in this place." Jo peers up at the trees. "It's hard to see already."

"We better hurry," Apollo says.

They step up and around fallen trees and rotting stumps, make their way through thick thimbleberry and snakeroot, shagbark and hornbeam. Jo's toe catches on a rock, and she stumbles forward, grabbing at a branch of prickly ash. "Ouch!" she cries, rubbing her hand on her shorts.

"Hurrying is not happening," Pirate Girl says.

"Maybe we should find a safe place to stay for the night before it gets too dark to find one," Henry says.

"Stay for the night?" Apollo's eyes go wide.

"Getting back down the mountain this way won't be like taking the road. We have to navigate. And there's no way we'll be able to find our way after the sun goes down. Vlad's men won't see us, but *we* won't see us, either," Pirate Girl says.

"That would definitely be the worst thing," Henry says. "Let's keep walking south until we find a clearing to make camp." Now that Henry remembers page 136 of his handbook, more and more is coming back to him. The perfect campsite, for instance. It's open. It's gently sloped, so that any rainwater might drain downward. It's near a water source, and has shelter from the prevailing winds, with trees to the west and north but not directly overhead.

It's strange, but for a moment, even with the darkening forest surrounding him, Henry feels the quiet confidence that knowledge brings. Knowledge is even better than luck, you see. And he feels that little flame again, too. That flicker of courage. That warm, bright light of his own true self. He remembers what his grandfather said: *I learned—as we all do in terrible times—who I really* am. Henry wonders if this is what he meant.

"Follow me," Pirate Girl says, and they follow. There's the snap and crack underfoot, and they must duck under low branches and maneuver through more and more thick underbrush. It looks the same in every direction. A clearing of any kind doesn't even seem possible. There are so many trees above and around that uneasiness edges in. Are they *all* trees? Regular, normal, *silent* trees?

"Water," Jo says. "I hear water."

They stop. Button is panting hard, and Henry is thirsty, too. Apollo has squishy envelopes of juice in his pack, but Henry knows that a water source is crucial in the wilderness.

"Rushing water," Henry says. "This way."

They fight their way forward, stepping over some things

and climbing under other things and freeing themselves from the jabby spines that grab at their sleeves and scratch the bare skin of their legs.

But Henry can see it: a little wedge of sky. It's the golden yellow of twilight.

And there it is—the almost-perfect campsite that his handbook describes. An open area of grassy moss, sheltered by a ring of trees, right near a fast-moving creek. Henry suddenly feels exhausted. All of the day has caught up to him. Or maybe all of his life so far.

"Where will we sleep?" Jo asks.

"We'll make a shelter out of my tarp, won't we, Henry?" Pirate Girl asks.

"You have a tarp?"

She takes a small square of plastic from her pants pocket and unfolds it. It's a wide, paint-splattered tarp with splotches of yellow and red.

A Paint-Spattered Tarp with Splotches of Yellow and Red

"My father used it to paint the garage," she says.

A feeling so large rushes in that Henry has no words for it. Pirate Girl and her scout readiness . . . She's made him speechless with admiration and respect. "Wow," he says again. It's all he can manage, but it's enough. She beams. He can see the sparkle of pride even in that dimming light.

"Well, it looks like we're going to have Monster Munchies and Salt-Freckled Zappers for dinner," Apollo says.

CHAPTER 30

A Long, Dark Night

It could be worse. In fact, for Henry, it often *has* been worse, much worse, under his own roof. Here, no one is shouting at him. No one's big mean face is in his. It's almost peaceful. Overhead, there's a tarp splattered with yellow and red, fastened to homemade pegs that Henry carved using a sapling and Pirate Girl's knife. And in front of them, there's a small fire with rocks around it that Henry built himself, and lit himself, using a rock, the file of Pirate Girl's knife, and a bit of her red pirate handkerchief that he tore off with his teeth. He tied Apollo's backpack up into a tree, too, so that no animals could reach their food source.

The fire spits sparks and crackles and glows a cozy, hot orange. Button lies across Henry's feet as the best dogs do. In the vast sky stretched out before them, the stars twinkle.

But what's *most* wonderful and magical is that Henry isn't lonely. He sits shoulder to shoulder with Pirate Girl, Apollo, and Jo under that tarp canopy. It gives him the best feeling ever, one that starts at his toes and fills him through and through.

Still, it's dark now.

It's dark, and there are dark, foresty sounds, strange noises, and weird shufflings in the nearby brush. There are the eerie calls of who-knows-what animal. The children edge closer to one another, warming their hands by the little fire. Creatures are likely peering at them with their glowing night eyes. It's even more frightening to imagine Needleman popping out as they sit together in those deep, shadowy woods.

"My mom is going to be so worried," Jo says. It's just like her to be concerned about other people, Henry thinks. Jo's eyes glimmer with the flames, and a tiny sliver of moonlight catches her hair.

"Our parents will be worried, too," Apollo says, though Rocco has long been asleep in one of Apollo's shoes, on a bed of grass that Jo tucked inside.

"What I'd give for a cheeseburger right about now," Pirate Girl says.

"Or a delicious bowl of Sturgeon Soufflé," Apollo adds.

"Or something from my mother's restaurant," Jo says. "A Monte Cristo sandwich. A lovely dish of clams casino. Salmon à la Chambord."

"Well, there are two last Yummers Without Cheese we can all share." Apollo hands them around.

Henry's cheeks are rosy from the fire. In spite of his small

Salmon à la Chambord

shoulders and bony knees and terrible circumstances, he has something important to say. "I know that Rocco is still a naked lizard. But we were all very brave today."

"Especially you, Pirate Girl, hanging off the edge of that cage." Jo gives Pirate Girl's shoulder a squeeze.

"It was no big deal." Pirate Girl shrugs. "But you, Jo. You were as fearless as Manuela Sáenz when she stopped the assassination of Simón Bolívar with her very own body." Pirate Girl remembers Jo's oral report, too.

"Apollo, *you* helped Rocco at our most horrible moment," Jo says.

"But it was Henry who kept encouraging all of us to go on," Apollo says. "You were prepared and loyal and lifesaving, Henry."

Henry smiles. He isn't used to getting compliments, and this is the highest Ranger Scout compliment you can get.

His happiness is like a giant balloon lifting up. "We've been . . . *spell breakers*, even if we haven't broken a spell," he says.

"Spell breakers," they all say at the same time, as if they're at a dinner, making a toast with fancy glasses of a bubbling drink, instead of sitting under a wedge of tarp, scared out of their wits.

They're quiet again. There's the rustling and snapping and cracking of the forest at night. Odd chirps. The cry of animals about to be eaten. They inch closer together. All that blackness out there makes every dark thought crawl in.

"When we shook Vlad's hand . . . ," Jo remembers with a shiver.

"I felt badness going through my whole body," Apollo says. Henry looks at Apollo, and when he does, he gets that same feeling of doom he had when Apollo rode through the shadow in Huge Meadow. Apollo's words make Henry feel terrible, like something awful is coming, but it's only regular Apollo.

"We shouldn't talk about this now, right before we go to sleep," Jo says.

"There's no way I'll be able to sleep out here," Apollo says. "It's too creepy and dark."

Jo pulls her knees to her chest, sets her cheek on them. "I just don't think I can keep my eyes open a moment longer. Fighting evil and nearly losing your life are really tiring."

"I'm keeping my eyes open all night," Apollo says.

Before Henry knows it, though, Apollo's head has drooped, and then he curls up like a croissant. Now only Henry and Pirate Girl are still awake. He remembers her holding on to that cage, her hands gripping with all her might, her face shiny with tears. It jabs his heart all over again.

"It *was* a big deal, Pirate Girl, hanging off the edge of that cage," he whispers, so as not to wake the others. "I don't know how you did it. You hardly seemed scared at all."

She looks at him. Her eyes are two bright planets in the firelight. "I *was* scared. I just held on anyway."

Before he even thinks it through, Henry says, "I'm scared all the time. And *I* just hold on anyway."

The words hang in the darkness for every owl and bullfrog and nightjar to see, and Henry gets that horrible, deep embarrassment, the one that makes him sure he's just wrecked everything. Oh why oh why oh why did he tell her that? But Pirate Girl only takes his hand. "I guess that makes us especially brave. I'm glad we're friends, Henry."

Friends. Friends! He can hardly believe it. He confessed a terrible truth, and he's still sitting here in one piece, and now he has a *friend!*

"Me too," Henry says. The *me* and *too* hold hands and dance in a circle together. What an astonishing day it's been.

Soon, Pirate Girl drifts off. Everyone, even Button, is slumped and drowsing. But Henry is still awake. He tries to relax but can't. He listens to the burbling creek and pretends that it's the lovely tones of an accordion. He tries to think up all of the varieties of fish he can, and then names all of the important rivers of the world: the Amazon, the Yangtze, the Nile.

The Nile

Wow, it's dark. So dark that it's almost like the moon has disappeared. He feels the thud of an ache, and he wonders if he'll ever see his grandfather again. When you're the only one awake in the middle of the night, you have thoughts like this. And when you're the only one awake in the middle of the night in a deep forest, you hear every shivery sound and have every shivery thought. You see, the problem is, Henry is used to keeping one ear open for angry footsteps. He's used to not entirely sleeping when danger is all around. So he does the job he knows. He stays alert. He worries for the world. He listens carefully. He looks around for anything that might harm them.

And that's when he sees it. Something the opposite of harm, something calm and beautiful—a rock. The most beautiful rock in the world maybe. Henry can see its beauty even in that darkness. It glows with the same luminescence of the moon above him, which he now realizes hasn't disappeared after all. He reaches for that rock, and holds it in his palm. The rock is even better than his lost lucky marble, because if knowledge is better than luck, then this glow is better than both. The glow is a reminder of the things you fear you've lost but will never lose—the moon, and light, and love.

He rubs it with his thumb to calm his nerves. The glow is almost warm. He's thankful for every small, smooth, beautiful thing that brings comfort. He finally falls into a dream.

Every dream of Henry's, though, is a dream where a part of him is still watchful. And that's why it is Henry and Henry alone who hears that crack of a branch in the early hours of dawn, when it is still dark but the sun is just beginning to lift. It's that hour when raccoons stumble home after a night out, and snakes make their final nocturnal slithers back to their caves, and bats swoop and grab at every last insect.

When the children, every single one of them except for Henry, continue to sleep peacefully, forgetting all about the danger they're in.

CHAPTER 31

The Worst Morning Ever

Henry suddenly stirs. He sits up. He has that terrible waking-up feeling one gets after a very bad day, when the memory of where you are and what has happened hits you with a sickening blast. He's in a forest. Apollo and Pirate Girl and Jo and Rocco and even Button are asleep around him. His neck feels like it's been stomped on by an especially large and cranky rhino.

An Especially Large and Cranky Rhino

Did he hear something? He thought he heard something. A crack. The crack of a branch.

Henry listens.

No. A bird chirps. The nearby creek rushes. Rocks under the creek water tumble.

Wait.

Wait just a minute.

The slightest rustle.

How he knows it's a bad rustle, well, who can say. He just does. Henry understands danger. It flows through his blood and grows along with his bones. And now his whole body fills with a sense of emergency. Button also knows, because an instinct for peril is handed down to every animal from the ones who came before. She startles awake, too. Her ears fold back. A low growl starts in her throat.

Henry shakes his friends. "Guys. Guys! Wake up," he whispers. Pirate Girl stretches and blinks. Apollo rouses and sits. Henry grabs a sleepy Rocco from the shoe and hides him in his shirt. Jo opens her eyes and stares straight ahead and sucks in her breath.

An acorn hits Henry's foot.

"Good morning, children," Mr. Reese the squirrel says.

Imagine the worst thing you could ever wake up to in the whole world, and then imagine something even worse yet.

It's over.

They've been found.

CHAPTER 32

The Untrustworthy Mr. Reese

Except . . . Maybe it's not over.

"Wait," Pirate Girl says. "You're talking."

"Of course I'm talking," Mr. Reese says.

"What about *chee chee chee*?" Apollo asks. He's quite skilled at squirrel impersonation on top of everything else.

"That's what squirrels say. I, however, am a man."

"Where's Needleman?" Pirate Girl asks. "Is he right behind you, coming any second?"

"Of course not. He's snug in his narrow little bed. I came out here to find you on my own."

"Why?" Apollo says. "So you can tell Needleman you found us? Or report back to Vlad Luxor?"

"Good gracious, no! I don't want *either of them* finding you! I'm here to guide you down the mountain! Do you know how much danger you're in?"

"Of course we know how much danger we're in!" Pirate Girl snaps. "Do you think we slept in a forest to enjoy the majesties of nature?"

"Why are you really here?" Apollo asks. "What do you want from us?"

"What do I want? I can't believe I have to spell this out to spell breakers!" Mr. Reese sits on his creepy squirrel haunches. "*I want* you to get off this mountain. *I want* you to stay away from Needleman so that you can break spells and eventually defeat Vlad Luxor."

"No one can defeat Vlad Luxor!" Apollo says.

"It *is* possible."

"How?" Henry asks.

"*I* don't know how! I assume it has something to do with goodness and bravery. Goodness is *always* the biggest threat to evil. But don't ask me. Ask your grandfather! He not only broke spells, he also defeated Avar Slaven," Mr. Reese says.

"He did?" Henry feels a swell of pride.

"He did. And before him, there were the spell breakers who conquered Dread Quill, and Cad Devon, and Gradion Fortrex—"

"If we're able to defeat him, does this mean we have nothing to fear from Vlad Luxor?" Jo asks.

"Don't be ridiculous! You have plenty to fear! He may zap you for a regular offense that annoys him, even if he doesn't find out who you are. And if he *does* find out who you are? Well, first Needleman will be swiftly dealt with, and then each of you will. Poof, poof, poof, poof, and POOF. No one will be left to undo *anything*. Your best chance is to get out of here immediately and to make sure you never find your-selves alone with Needleman again. Gather your things and let's get going."

"You're going to guide us down the mountain," Jo says. She doesn't sound too sure.

"I am."

"It's a trap," Apollo says. "I know a trap when I hear one."

"Trap." Rocco's muffled voice comes from the inside of Henry's shirt.

"Why would you help us?" Pirate Girl says. "Out of the goodness of your revolting and disgusting little rodent heart?"

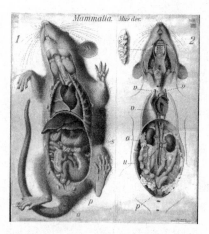

Revolting and Disgusting Little
Rodent Heart, Fig. 1 and 2

"Of course not!" Mr. Reese says. "I was Vlad Luxor's left-hand man! You shouldn't even trust me! I have very little goodness in my heart. I am only helping you so that you can help *me. You* are the only ones who can turn me from a squirrel back into a man."

"That's right. We are," Pirate Girl says, as if there were a hundred other things she'd rather turn him into.

"As soon as you find out how, you're going to return me to the handsome, intelligent, quick-witted, agile, athletic, and bushy-haired gent I was. Unless you'd rather that I scurry off right now and tell Needleman that I found you . . ."

"We'll do it, Mr. Reese!" Henry says.

"Good. Now, will you all please hurry it up? Be quick like little squirrels." Mr. Reese claps his creepy little hands. *"Chee chee chee."*

CHAPTER 33

The Nasty Surprise
in the Center of the Road

As the sun rises in the sky, the forest leaves turn a yellow-ish pink and then a lush green, and the boughs of the trees glisten and twinkle with morning dew. Henry feels in his pocket to make sure his rock is still there as Mr. Reese leads them down the bank of the creek. They step across fallen logs and leap from boulder to boulder so as not to get their shoes wet. They follow the curves and bends of the flowing water, which catches the morning rays and makes the river a sea of diamonds. They stop only to get a drink. Button gulps for a good, long time. The water is cold and delicious. It feels like drinking the just-melted ice from the grand peaks of the world's tallest mountain, somewhere in the Jaggeds.

Rocco rides on the back of Button. Apollo's cheekbones are high, and he's handsome even at this early hour, and Henry swears Apollo's shoulders have broadened overnight. Jo keeps up with Mr. Reese, eager to get home to let her

The World's Tallest Mountain,
Somewhere in the Jaggeds

mother know she's safe. Pirate Girl stays with Henry, bring-
ing up the rear. She looks like something is worrying her.

"Rocco—" she finally says.

Henry has the same worry. "I know."

"He hasn't hidden in plain sight of Vlad Luxor yet," she
says.

"How can we be spell breakers if he's still a naked lizard?"

"I have no idea, Henry." Pirate Girl shakes her head. It's
good to have a friend to share your troubles with.

In spite of their concerns, Henry can tell that they're getting closer to the ground. The slope levels, and even his surroundings begin to look familiar. In the far-off distance, he
recognizes a certain hill of their town. He'd know that hill
anywhere. Henry always thought it resembled the side view
of a buffalo.

And then, Mr. Reese stops.

"Wait here," he says. "We're approaching the iron wall and

The Side View of a Buffalo

the gate. Vlad's men are lazy and they sleep late, but let me make sure the coast is clear. When I give the signal, go! Run! Head back to your houses. And back to your grandfather, Henry Every, so the lot of you can learn how to return me to manhood."

They hide in a thick patch of trees near the road, standing close enough together that Henry can almost hear their hearts beating. Or maybe that's just his own, thumping away in his chest with the deepest hope that this horrible mountain will soon be behind them.

"I'm scared," Jo says.

"We're almost home," Pirate Girl tells her.

In a moment, Mr. Reese returns, waving his little arms.

"All right. *Now,*" Jo says.

They run. Henry's thin legs pump hard. Button flies as Rocco holds tight to her collar. Pirate Girl's pockets clang and bang with the last of her stuff. The gate is up ahead. It seems so long ago that they first passed through it. They just need to get to the other side, and then through the Y and the meadow, and back into town.

Mr. Reese is gesturing madly.

But then, he does something strange. Just before they reach the gates, Mr. Reese veers off the path and scurries frantically up a cypress, as if he's avoiding an oncoming truck.

It is *not* an oncoming truck.

It's Vlad Luxor, standing right in the center of the road.

CHAPTER 34

Two Most Unfortunate Misunderstandings

C *hee chee chee,"* Mr. Reese says from the tree branch above them. *"CHEE CHEE CHEE!"*

"You traitor!" Pirate Girl hisses.

"I'm not a traitor," Mr. Reese hiss-whispers back. "I am plenty of other things, but not that! You were supposed to wait for the *signal*!"

"Wasn't that the signal?" Apollo says.

"Of course that wasn't the signal! Do you think that would be the signal when YOU KNOW WHO is right there?"

"Oh no," Jo says. "Oh no, oh no, oh no."

"What is he doing?" Apollo asks.

It *is* strange. Vlad Luxor is walking back and forth, back and forth, across the road in front of the open gate. He seems to be looking for something and speaking to someone.

He's clad in only his boxers, which are lime green and decorated with many little images of Vlad. On his feet, he is wearing a pair of lovely slippers made out of yarn.

Lovely Slippers
Made Out of Yarn

While it's true that Vlad looks a little silly, with his white flesh and his large tummy and his mouth turned down in a pout, there is nothing silly, nothing funny at all, about the horrific damage he's done and the hurt he's caused. And the *additional* damage he can do right this minute. Henry gets that same curling feeling of fear and disgust. Once again, he is suddenly cold. So cold that the chill seems to sink into the farthest reaches of his body. Apollo whimpers. Pirate Girl rubs her arms and shivers as if it's winter.

"Good MORNING," Vlad Luxor says. "GOOD morning. Good mooorning. Gooood morning!"

He's practicing, Henry realizes. Talking to an imaginary audience. And then Henry realizes something else. Pirate Girl meets his eyes, because she does, too.

"Rocco," they both whisper in Button's direction, where Rocco sits on the dog's back.

"Now is your chance, Rocco," Henry whispers. "Now is *really* your chance. Be very good and very quiet and hide in plain sight. All we have to do is walk respectfully by. Can you do this?"

Rocco's small green head nods.

Jo's hand slips into Apollo's. Pirate Girl takes Henry's. Henry's head begins to throb. His stomach has knotted up like the worst tangle of Christmas lights.

The Worst Tangle of Christmas Lights

As the children step forward, Henry feels the sparks of panic all the way to his fingers and toes. They walk humbly and politely to the other side of the gate, *their* side, where Vlad Luxor paces. At least they're past those horrible looming doors of iron leaves and vines.

"Where is my newspaper?" Vlad Luxor says to them.

"Newspaper, sir?" Henry thinks maybe it's best if he speaks. He's the one who's most used to talking to large and frightening people.

"Newspaper! That heavy, folded lump of lies printed on pulp! It is going to have lots of words and pictures about my parade and fair of yesterday."

"I don't know, sir. I've never seen one of those before."

"Hmph," he says. "Maybe I got rid of them."

Vlad looks at Henry. And then he looks at the other children. "Who are you happy little ones? You look familiar to me. Do you look familiar to me?"

"We were at your wonderful fair yesterday. And your astonishing parade," Henry says.

"Yes?" Vlad beams. His white skin quivers like raw chicken.

"It was incredible," Henry says. "And glorious. And magnificent." He's trying to think of all the biggest and best words.

"It was the best day of your life, I'm certain," Vlad Luxor says.

"Oh, definitely." *Please don't notice Button,* Henry silently begs. *Please don't notice Rocco.*

"And who is this very small unshaven man?" Vlad Luxor asks.

"That's Button, my dog," Henry says.

Pirate Girl makes that terrible, terrible *ckkk* sound in her throat. Henry knows it's a nervous laugh, but still! He shoots her a warning look. If she cracks up with uncontrollable hilarity now, it's over for all of them.

"He's an awfully *silent* small unshaven man," Vlad Luxor says. "How rude."

"He's just too awed by your presence to speak, sir. I'm barely able to do it myself," Henry says.

"What is that spot?" Vlad Luxor says. "I believe there's something crawling on the furry man! Uck! Horror of horrors! It's a blechy little reptile!"

It's over. It's really, really over. Vlad Luxor is staring straight at Rocco. Now he leans down to look right into Rocco's tiny face.

And that's when the worst of *all* the worst things happens.

Rocco's tongue slips out of his mouth.

"Did you see that?" Vlad says in shock.

Of course Henry saw that! "I'm not sure what you mean, sir."

"He stuck his tongue out at me."

Apollo drops Jo's hand and steps forward. "It wasn't a sign of disrespect, sir," he butts in nervously. "He's a lizard. Lizards use their tongues to smell things. They catch scent particles all along here—" Apollo sticks out his own tongue and points to its sides.

"HE STUCK OUT HIS TONGUE, TOO!" Vlad booms. "I will not tolerate PEOPLE MAKING FUN OF ME! I will not stand for LITTLE BRATS TRYING TO GET ATTENTION!"

Henry flinches at the shrill fury in Vlad Luxor's voice. His shoulders hunch in self-protection, same as when his father explodes in rage, and he turns away and shuts his eyes hard in fear.

And when Henry finally opens them again and sees what he sees, he feels like his life is over.

Next to Button and Rocco, where Apollo had been standing, there is a second naked lizard.

CHAPTER 35

What Happens Next

That'll teach you, you nasty child," Vlad Luxor says. He steps to the other side of the gate and flings it shut, where it rattles with an enormous and final banging clang. He shuffles back up the road in his slippers. A sob escapes Jo's throat. Henry looks and sees tears streaming down her lovely face.

"This is awful," Pirate Girl says. "Awful, awful, awful! This situation cannot get worse."

"And Rocco was doing such a terrific job, too," Jo cries. "And Apollo was only trying to explain!"

"When the lizard puts his tongue back in," Apollo says in the tiniest naked lizard voice, "it hits the roof of his mouth, where there is an organ that acts essentially like a *nose*— Wait. My hands. My *legs*. You are all suddenly so very *tall*."

"Oh, Apollo," Henry cries.

"You children!" Mr. Reese shouts from the tree. Henry had forgotten all about him. "Get out of here! Hurry, before

Needleman arrives and finishes off the rest of you! Don't stand here crying like a bunch of weenies!"

A Bunch of Weenies

"He's right," Pirate Girl says. "We've got to go."

"I am so sorry, Henry!" tiny Apollo says. "Vlad Luxor turned Button into a GIANT DOG!"

"Poor Apollo," Jo says.

"Stop whining and GET A MOVE ON," Mr. Reese yells.

Henry scoops up Apollo and sets him next to his brother. "Come on," he says. "We have to hurry."

Button takes off, and the children run and run, too, until Henry doesn't think he can run anymore. He is so, so tired. He has never been so tired in all his life, and may never be as tired again. He sees the Y up ahead. The familiar Y, where one road leads down to the sea, one up the mountain, and the other into town. He sees their bikes. It feels like it's been months and months since they saw them last.

They shouldn't stop. Needleman could be anywhere. He could be coming down the mountain right now, his pointed nose sniffing them out, the men with their scary faces and mutton-chop sideburns at his heels. But they are so exhausted and so defeated that nothing seems to matter. Henry drops to the grass. Jo drops next to him, and then Pirate Girl does, and so does Button. Through Huge Meadow, in the distance, Henry can see the little lights of their town coming on, meaning that everyone is rising, meaning that it's a new day.

He wants to cry. He has failed so badly. Instead of returning to town with a naked lizard who's been turned back into a boy, he will be returning with two boys who've become naked lizards. He can only imagine the sorrow of Apollo's kind mother and good father. He can only imagine the silence that will come from their house in the evenings, when there used to be laughter.

"Wait," Apollo says. "Vlad Luxor has made all of *you* enormous, too."

"Apollo . . . ," Jo begins, but she can't bear to finish.

"Oh no," Apollo says. He flicks his tongue out. "Oh no. I do believe I just smelled a dandelion with the roof of my mouth. No. No, no, no, no, NO!" Apollo begins to cry. Tears fall from the globes of his reptile eyes and down his green triangle face.

And then, *Rocco* begins to cry. They are clutching each other and sobbing, two brothers, two naked lizards, and it is the saddest sight you could ever see in your life.

"Bad," Rocco cries. "I'm a bad, bad boy."

Oh, it's awful. It makes Henry feel so terrible that he puts his hand in his pocket for the most beautiful rock in the world. He holds it in his palm. Everything seems lost. If he ever needed a reminder that everything is *never* lost, it's now.

"No, Rocco," Pirate Girl says. "No you're not."

"No you're not, Rocco," Jo says, too.

"Bad boy," he cries.

To see Rocco like that . . . Henry has no words for it. It crushes him. He's felt this same way himself before—small and ashamed. Like this is all his fault, when it's really only Vlad Luxor's fault. He knows how much it *hurts*. And he thinks, too, about *why* Rocco has been trying so hard to get attention lately. It's maybe even understandable.

"You're not a bad boy, Rocco," Henry says softly. "Your mom just had a new baby. Otto was getting all the attention. You just wanted everyone to notice you. To *see* you."

Rocco stops crying. His bulgy eyes blink. "When you're small, it's hard to know how to tell people what you need," Henry continues. "It's hard to have the words. It's easier to poke and copy and sing annoying songs. You're not bad, Rocco. I know how you must feel. You're not bad for being little."

It is hard to even describe what happens next. It is so sudden, and so miraculous, and so alarming for poor Button. All at once, with Henry's words, two boys are piled on top of the small Jack Russell terrier, who is squirming and wiggling to be free.

Two *boys.*

"Apollo?" Henry can't believe his eyes. He's so stunned that he forces himself to blink and look again. "Rocco?"

It *is* Rocco, the little-boy Rocco. With the bruised knees and sticky face and brown eyes and tousled hair, not the Rocco with the ancient skin and bulgy orbs of a reptile. And neither one of them is naked, either, much to Henry's great shock and relief. Apollo is wearing the clothes he had on just a few moments ago. Rocco is wearing a pair of shorts and his favorite T-shirt that features a serious yet adorable carrier pigeon.

"I'm here," Rocco says in a little-boy voice.

"Henry," Jo breathes. "Henry, Henry, Henry!" She's looking at him as if he's the most amazing thing in the world. She can barely speak. "How did you do it? How did this happen?"

"I don't know," Henry says. He can't understand it himself.

A Serious Yet Adorable Carrier Pigeon

All at once, Apollo is hugging him, and so is Jo, and Pirate Girl, and Rocco. Henry is in a great big muddle of hugs and arms and triumph and disbelief. "Maybe we really *are* spell breakers," Henry says from the center of it all.

CHAPTER 36

The Broken Bed

Well, you can imagine the celebrations that ensue. The incredible, glorious, magnificent, yet somewhat *secret* celebrations. When the children arrive back in town with Rocco *the boy*, Jo's mother runs from Rio Royale with tears of relief on her face. The diners with their napkins in their collars run out, too, and grip each other's elbows with elation and renewed hope. Jo is kissed at least a hundred times, and then she twists free. There is a very, very important thing they all must do, a reunion that none of them want to miss. After the most solemn promise that she'll return by dinner, the children retrieve their bikes. They pedal as fast as they can to the Dante house as Rocco, the little boy, runs ahead with one shoe untied.

When he spots them out the window, Mr. Dante flings open the door with joy, and Mrs. Dante sobs with the greatest happiness. She clutches her sons to her, and smooches them again and again. *Five* children and one dog are ushered in quickly, out of sight, and fed the most incredible treats,

220

since they're starving. The cupboard doors are tossed open. Anything they want is theirs. Peanut Bloats and Crispy Tots, Nugget Crumples and Cherry Freezees and Fruity Zingers. Button receives an entire plate of Meat with Beef. When her tummy is satisfyingly full, the brave but weary terrier finds a warm circle of sun on the Dantes' kitchen floor and does what she most wants to do—sleep.

Now that they are bursting with the fabulous, shooting energy of victory plus enormous amounts of sugar and salt, sleep is the last thing the children want. They have no idea how they undid the spell, but right then, it doesn't matter a bit. They blare the television and plink on toy pianos and jump on the Dantes' extravagantly large bed. Every single one of them is holding hands in a circle and jumping with wild delight—Apollo and Rocco and Jo and Pirate Girl and Henry, too, of course. But so is little sister Coco, and baby Otto, who is mostly a wobbly blop, bouncing about in the center. Coco has eaten all the green Fruity Zingers that everybody hates because they taste like a bad burrito. Her tongue and teeth are green, and baby Otto crawls and drools, and Rocco hits Apollo and Apollo calls him a donkey and pinches him, and Henry has never been so happy. He is holding hands with Jo on one side and Pirate Girl on the other, and all of them, all of his *friends*, are going up and down and up and down in demented happiness and shrieking, "Yay, yay, yay!" at the top of their lungs, loud enough to test any parent's nerves. And then there is an awful *crack* and *galumph* as the end corner of the bed crashes down.

"Uh-oh. I think we broke something," Apollo says, and plops down. Baby Otto crawls over and sits on Apollo's head, and then the rest of them plop down, too. Now the bed tilts as dangerously as the Leaning Tower of Pisa.

The Leaning Tower of Pisa

From the high end of the bed, Pirate Girl gives Henry a shy look. He has a surprising thought right then: She is quite astonishing, he realizes, and not just because she's got the most incredible pocketknife he's ever seen. Her strength gives her a distinct glow.

"What's happening in here?" Mrs. Dante says, peeking in through the door. "I heard a rather large crack and a big crash. Oh, I see. The bed."

"Large crack," Rocco says, and pokes Apollo in the butt. This sends Coco into a fit of giggles. Henry starts to giggle, too. It's that *ckkk* sound again, because he's afraid they're in big, big trouble.

But Mrs. Dante only shakes her head and smiles. And then she does something remarkable. She tousles Henry's hair.

She hugs his shoulders. With her thumb, she gently points out a splotch of Cherry Freezee on his cheek. His heart is so, so full.

"Beloveds," Mrs. Dante says.

● ◐ ○

In town, the whispers have already started.

Spell breakers, Ms. Esmé Silvooplay, the baker, murmurs to Miss Becky, from Creamy Dreamy Dairy. *Spell breakers,* Sir Loinshank Jr. of Big Meats utters to Vic Chihuahua, his neighbor. *Spell breakers, spell breakers,* everyone says.

"Spell breaker? Hmph," Mrs. Every says to Henry when he and Button finally arrive back home that evening. "Maybe this means we'll one day forgive you for the broken window we had to repair."

"After you pay for it with your allowance," Mr. Every says.

"I don't get an allowance," Henry says.

"Well, you can pay for it with the loads of money you'll charge to turn all those pathetic sparrows and snakes and trees back into people again," Mrs. Every says.

"Ugh, I knew he was a lot like my father," Mr. Every says from his chair, which, for a brief moment, Henry imagines is not a chair but something else.

That night, Henry and Button must sneak downstairs and nibble on the last leftover shreds of an overcooked pork chop. It is as tough and dry as the grossest recycled cereal box. But it's all right. That night it is, anyway. Henry's tummy is still full from the extravagant amount of treats at the Dante house.

In his room, Henry opens his brand-new window. He sticks his head out and breathes in the sweet night smell of summer. He can see the yellow light from one of the Dantes' windows, and he can see the large, luminescent moon, which he slept under only the night before. He can feel that little flame inside his own chest.

Finally, he gets into his small iron bed with the thin mattress. Button hops up next to him. Henry retrieves his *Ranger Scout*

*Not a Chair but
Something Else*

Handbook, sixth edition, from the corner of his closet and puts it back under his pillow. He folds his fingers around the most beautiful rock in the world and shuts his eyes. And on this night, because friendship can hold you, and light can carry you, and knowledge can lead you, and also because bravery can just plain wear you out, he sleeps as hard as a stone.

CHAPTER 37

A Delicious Feast

Of course, the biggest celebration of all comes the very next day, when the children get back on their bikes and ride once more through the meadow, past the Circle of the Y, and then to the left, down, down toward the ocean. It's still quite nerve-racking, as you can imagine, since Needleman might be lurking anywhere, and since Apollo's new walkie-talkie cackles every few minutes as his parents check to see if they're all right. The children pedal madly, until they smell the glorious and deep smells of salt water and seaweed, plus the dead stuff that dogs like to roll in. Button rides in Pirate Girl's sidecar, and Jo's hair flies behind her, and Apollo is on his bike minus Rocco, who is at home doing the things little boys sometimes do—poke their sisters, ask again and again if they can jump on the trampoline without their mothers watching, cry very loudly and annoyingly when told no.

The sky gets larger as they get nearer to the sea. First, Henry sees the twinkle of water. And then, with relief and gladness, he spots the tip of Grandfather's house, lit in the day *and* in the night, so that you can hear its message at any hour. *Blink,* the lighthouse says, *there's a safe place in the world. Blink, you won't be lost forever. Blink, you are never as alone as you feel.*

They ditch their bikes and run up the porch steps. The door opens, and there he is—Captain Every, in his crisp and magnificent blue uniform. His white beard is trimmed, and his buttons gleam. Grandfather's eyes are both calm and delighted, which fills Henry with that warm feeling of safety and shelter.

"Ah! The valiant and daring children plus one dog are here, my dearest!" he calls. "Come and see the little ones with the right stuff!"

The Beautiful Librarian rushes to the door now, too. She stands behind Captain Every, her smile as bright as the lighthouse itself. She's wearing a dress of green satin, which looks ravishing. Her hair is piled atop her head like a dollop of the most perfect whipped cream.

"Come and have something to eat," The Beautiful Librarian says.

The Most Perfect Whipped Cream

Oh, how Henry loves those words, especially now that he's back home, where there are only expired tins of oily fish and cellophane tubes with the last stale crackers no one else wants. In the dining room, there's a feast. There is beef bourguignon. There is chicken à la king. There is a crown roast of frankfurters, and a colorful ring of gelatin and pimentos. There are warm, buttery bread rolls as squishy as pillows, and creamy, rich cheeses, and slices of juicy, exotic fruits. But best of all, there is a tall white cake suitable for a wedding.

Grandfather lifts his water glass, and the ice tinkles merrily. "Let's have a toast." They lift their glasses. "To generations of spell breakers, to the light in the darkness, to the triumph of good over evil, to—"

A Tall White Cake Suitable for a Wedding

"Cheers," The Beautiful Librarian says. She smells like a field of wildflowers that has suddenly bloomed.

"There is so much I don't understand," Jo says.

"Me either," Pirate Girl says.

"Same here," Apollo agrees.

"Especially about the spell," Henry adds. "Rocco never *did* hide in plain sight."

"Are you all finished with your meals?" Captain Every asks, removing the napkin from under his chin and dabbing at a spot on his blue captain's jacket.

"One more buttery roll," Pirate Girl says. "Can you pass them, Henry?" He does, and she takes one from the plate.

"Yes, but what about the cake?" Apollo asks. It is still sitting tall and unsliced. Apollo is maybe not using his best manners asking this question, but Henry wonders the same thing.

Captain Every doesn't answer. "Please check the periscope," he says to The Beautiful Librarian, who looks through the mounted contraption in the corner of the dining room. It resembles a pair of binoculars connected to a long tube, which disappears through the ceiling, travels up two levels of rooms, and then pops through the roof.

"A periscope!" Apollo says. "I read about those in *The Great History of the Royal Navy*! They allow submarines to search for threats on the surface of the water while remaining submerged."

The Beautiful Librarian swivels it to the left and then to the right.

"All clear," she says to the captain.

"Excellent! Let's go to the library for the answers to some important questions."

CHAPTER 38

The Children Turn the Page

As you know, it has been a terrible, frightening, exhila-rating, and triumphant few days. And there has been a relieving but confusing outcome. But the children are entering one of the most magical places in the world: a library. Not just any library, either, but a library that swirls upward in a lighthouse, where one brilliant beam steadily shines, in any kind of darkness, danger, or storm.

There are thousands upon thousands of beautiful, astonishing books, and so, before getting down to business, the children stare from the bottom up, and race to the top to look down, at the books, at the sea stretching out, at the enormous lantern with its many-sided glass. Apollo tips the spines and smells the pages. Pirate Girl gazes at images of zebras and rockets, ancient pyramids, and mariner ships of old stuck in icebergs from the beginning of time.

Jo hugs an elaborate golden volume to her chest. Henry and Button look with wonder at the greatest hope they have against evil: knowledge and light.

Mariner Ship of Old Stuck in Iceberg
from the Beginning of Time

Finally, the *keeper* of the knowledge and the *keeper* of the light look at each other and nod. "It's time," The Beautiful Librarian says to Captain Every.

"Spells!" Grandfather calls in a big, booming voice. "Come and see, you wonderful, radiant children."

The Beautiful Librarian has the huge, leathery book of spells out again, open to a familiar page.

Henry can hardly wait. His heart thrums as fast as a hummingbird's. Answers are waiting. Stuff that will change other stuff. "We know all about this one. The Hiding in Plain Sight cure," Apollo says, bending down toward the open book before reading aloud. "'In the dreadful and appalling circumstance that option one and option two are not options, there is the optional option three. Victim must be paraded in full view of the spell caster without being seen.'"

"But one must always remember—" The Beautiful Librarian says.

"To turn the page," Pirate Girl says. She lifts the corner and sets one yellowed piece of paper against the next. They stare at the small words, which curve and loop with cramped elegance.

"'That's it. *Finiti, finuto,*'" Henry reads.

"That's it?" Pirate Girl says.

"'The end.'" Henry looks up.

"We turned the page. There's still no answer!" Apollo says.

"Ugh!" The Beautiful Librarian tosses up her hands in frustration. "Proving once again that you should always seek multiple sources, especially when it comes to evil. Stay right here."

She takes off. Grandfather removes his pocket watch from his jacket and keeps his eyes fixed on the second hand. Henry hears The Beautiful Librarian's feet running up the lighthouse stairs. "Not this, wait, maybe, well, no," they hear her muttering. "Just a minute!" she calls down to them.

Grandfather Every looks up from his pocket watch. "Never fear. The Beautiful Librarian is smart, strong, and prepared for anything. The best qualities," he says, and winks at Henry.

"*Nakedismo*, incantation, clarifications and elucidations . . . Yes! I knew there had to be an answer somewhere in these books. I found it!" she yells. Down the stairs she comes. She's out of breath, and her face is flushed. A lock of her beautifully dolloped hair has escaped and falls down her forehead.

Grandfather looks at his watch. "Three minutes, fifty-eight seconds. Extraordinary."

The Beautiful Librarian thunks the book onto the table. It's a different, smaller book, but just as ancient, and it smells like buried treasure that's been buried a century too long.

"Pee-yew," Apollo says.

The Beautiful Librarian holds her nose and reads. "'*Lizardo Nakedismo*. In the event of cataclysmic failure of optional options one through three, it is rumored that a last resort effort can be made using:

1. the tears of two lizards;
2. a great display of intelligence, bravery, belief, and understanding;
3. one of the most beautiful rocks in the world.'"

The Beautiful Librarian unplugs her nose. Henry looks up at his grandfather, and then he reaches into his pocket. "This?" It is indeed quite beautiful, glowing like a firefly in his cupped hand. "This is what undid the spell?"

Captain Every laughs. When he does, his eyes twinkle like the best snowflakes of winter. "Well, yes, that. But more importantly, *you* four broke the spell. The children with *the stuff*. And do you know *why* you have the stuff?"

"Because DNA is made up of chromosomes, and you get half of them from your father and half from your mo—"

"Because *you*, Apollo Dante, are from a long line of great thinkers and philosophers," Grandfather interrupts. "Challengers of the status quo. People who gather knowledge for greater understanding. *Spell breakers.*"

Apollo beams. "Like Grandmother Antonia," he says.

"And you, Josephine Idár," he says to Jo, "are from a long line of people who have fought for justice. Protesters, leaders. Righters of wrongs, who look after the less fortunate. *Spell breakers.*"

Jo smiles. "Manuela Sáenz, revolutionary hero of South America. And Aunt Maria Fernanda."

"That's right," Captain Every says, nodding, "and many others." He turns his gaze to Pirate Girl.

"I don't know," she says. "My father wasn't home to ask. A long line of pirates?"

Captain Every laughs again. The Beautiful Librarian and Captain Every catch eyes and exchange a knowing look. "No. Not pirates."

"Not pirates?" She sounds a little disappointed.

"Carson Curie Shackleton, also known as Pirate Girl, *you* are a descendant of many great and fearless explorers and scientists. Crossers of the oceans and the continents, wayfarers to the farthest-most corners of our planet, protectors of the earth, who seek to understand the universe as a whole. Who keep going forward when others stop.

Sometimes traveling solo, always traveling fierce and tenderhearted. *Spell breakers.*"

"I am?"

"You are."

Her face flushes. Henry can see her taking in this news and holding it close. He understands what this means for her. The land *and* the sea. Ships and sled dogs. The North and the South Poles, with all of the treacherous, magnificent space between. "I can hardly believe it," she says.

"*I* believe it." The Beautiful Librarian sets a hand on her shoulder.

"And you, Henry. You."

Now Grandfather Every turns to him. He takes Henry's small, thin hands in his large, warm, enveloping ones. He fixes his strong gaze right into Henry's eyes.

"Well, a long time ago, there was a bad seed, which means that sometimes there are more and more bad seeds. Regular bad seeds, with ordinary evil. And I'm sorry, son, I am so sorry that you live where parents roar at you, where rough hands shove, and stingy hands grab, and where you are hungry, and unseen, and afraid, always afraid, even when your eyes close at night."

Henry's throat gets tight. His eyes get watery with tears. He can't speak, so he only swallows and nods.

"It makes it hard to find the light inside, son. You have to dig down deep, so deep, to find it. You have to keep believing in it, when it's most hard to. I live here and you live there now, and that *there now* is awful. But you must remember, Henry. You must hold on to this with all your might: Awful is never permanent. Never. Never ever."

A tear escapes and wets Henry's cheek. He wipes it away with the back of his hand.

"Something else happens, too," Grandfather continues, "when you are someone who must listen and watch closely out of fear, waiting to see if a face is about to turn dark, or a voice is about to lower. When you know what it's like to feel sad, and bad, and alone. You develop a different, far greater skill. A skill I wish you didn't have already, but you do: an ability to truly see others. To understand what they might be feeling. To notice the things others sometimes don't, and to take things sincerely into your heart. It's a great power against evil, son, a great one, even if it doesn't always feel that way."

Henry sees that Pirate Girl's eyes are watering along with his. He feels so much that all of it gathers in his chest in a big ball. He feels so much that maybe he, like Rocco, is too small to have the words for it yet.

"And so you, Henry—you are from a long, long line, a line that shoots this way and that, of people who go through hard things without losing their hearts. People who see deeply, and understand deeply, and feel deeply. *Spell breakers.*"

Another tear drops down his face, and another drops down his nose, but Henry just lets them come. He lets his hands be held all warm in his grandfather's. He lets his eyes be held, too. It's like the best and safest rest you can imagine.

"You saw, Henry, you really *saw* who was there in front of you. A sad little boy, not a bad one. And *all* of you," Captain Every says, to Jo and Apollo and Pirate Girl and even Button. "Your desire to help others, your intelligence and kindness and bravery, your patience with an annoying naked lizard, your stand against evil . . . *That* is what brought the Dante family their joy again."

Jo clears her throat. Her eyes glisten with tears, too. And when she speaks, her voice is hoarse with emotion. "Henry? Thank you for being such a good friend. Thank you for being our not-a-bad-seed-but-the-best-seed *leader.*"

Now Jo does something amazing and incredible: She kisses Henry's cheek. The kiss, the spell, Grandfather and The Beautiful Librarian, Pirate Girl and Apollo and Button, these friends—the flicker of light is a blaze in Henry's chest.

"We're a *team* of spell breakers," Henry says. He feels so much, he can hardly talk. It's the happiest and least lonely he's ever been in his whole life. It seems as if he's reached the very mountaintop and gone to the farthest-most corner of *every* feeling, but of course he's wrong. In the coming days and years he will be much more miserable, and much, *much* more full of joy.

The Beautiful Librarian closes the book. But then Captain

Every taps the ancient cover with his fingers. "Of course, a closed book does not mean the end of the story."

"It doesn't?"

"Unfortunately and fortunately in equal measures. There are a few further matters we must discuss. Darling, will you kindly fetch the dusty bottle to the farthest right of the bottles?"

The Dusty Bottle to the Farthest
Right of the Bottles

"Big," The Beautiful Librarian says with a stern look and a small shake of her head.

"Ugh! Truly sorry, my darling. How could I forget? I'll be right back," he says.

CHAPTER 39

The Forward Clock

This time the liquid is a deep scarlet, and the bubbles are as large and clear as ice cubes. Pirate Girl holds her green glass and looks into it questioningly. Then she tips it down her throat.

"Holy gladioli! Surprisingly scrumptious." She covers her mouth with her napkin in a polite burp.

Jo sips. Henry takes a drink, feeling the big ruby bubbles on his tongue. If deep scarlet had a taste, this would be it. It's a rich and delectable combination of raspberry and cherry and every red fruit you can think of. He sets his hands around the glass.

Grandfather gulps his down and pours another.

"Those further matters we need to discuss?" Apollo reminds.

Grandfather removes his pocket watch and gazes down his nose at the second hand. "Not. Quite. Yet . . . All right. *Now.*"

Just as Grandfather tucks the watch back into his pocket, Henry hears the rumble of a truck coming up the road, and the sound of heavy tires on gravel. From the table, the children crane their necks, but it's hard to see out the window from there.

"I think it's the Big Meats truck," Jo says.

"Is that old man Loinshank getting out?" Apollo asks. "I see a bit of a white apron."

"Should I let him—" Henry begins to push back his chair, but Grandfather sets his large hand on Henry's arm.

"Wait. You'll see."

Henry hears a large clunk. Next, there's a knock at the old wooden door, causing Button to bark. There's the sound of footsteps retreating, and then the grumble of an engine starting up before the truck drives away.

"I wonder what it is today." The Beautiful Librarian heads toward the door. The children meet each other's eyes in question, but Henry remembers. Those gifts. The presents his grandfather some-times gets. In a moment, The Beautiful Librarian is back. She's carrying an ornate but somewhat garish mantel clock.

"Oof, this thing weighs a ton," she says, before setting it hard and heavy on the table.

"And its hands are

An Ornate but Somewhat Garish Mantel Clock

frozen at ten minutes before two," Pirate Girl notices. "It's almost that time now."

"This must have been in his family for generations," The Beautiful Librarian says. "Let me read the card." She opens a tiny square of butcher paper, taped to the clock. "'This was in my family for generations. Sir Loinshank Jr.'"

Grandfather sits back in his chair with his arms folded calmly across his large chest. "Do you understand, children?" he says. "Already this week there was a Chinese vase and a platter of marzipan fruits. The gifts are rolling in."

Henry *does* understand. His voice is solemn. "The people in the province know there will be a lot more spells to break."

"A lot more?" Apollo looks slightly ill.

"A lot more?" Pirate Girl looks slightly pleased.

"And we should discuss one last thing. A rather gigantic and hideous piece of business," Grandfather says.

"This is the part I'm *really* afraid to hear." Apollo hunches his shoulders up toward his ears.

"Well, you've likely guessed by now that you have an even larger job to do. The largest," Captain Every says.

"I can't even say his name. I am still shaking at the thought of him at that gate," Jo says.

Henry also shudders at the memory. But then he gets that confusing feeling where you are filled with excitement and dread at the same time, like when you stand at the edge of a diving board, or it's the first day of school, or you're about to try some grown-up food like Tuna Tofu.

"How are we supposed to defeat Vlad Luxor?" he asks.

"How? Well, with Avar Slaven, there was a secret code, a twist of latitude and longitude, many tormented, sleepless nights, an assortment of frightening yet amusing finger puppets—"

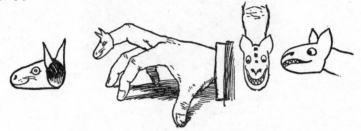

An Assortment of Frightening Yet Amusing Finger Puppets

"Big," The Beautiful Librarian says. "Maybe we should just stick with another next spell for now. Tell them about Mr. Terrence Tortellini."

"You're right as always. The first thing anyone must do if they want to change the future is to understand the past," Grandfather says.

Under the table, Apollo nudges Henry's foot and gives him an insistent stare. And Apollo has a point. There's *another* first thing to do before they attempt to change the future. "Um, Grandfather?" Henry asks.

"Yes, dear boy?" Henry loves when his grandfather calls him this.

"The cake?"

"Oh, heavens! I almost forgot. The tall white cake suitable for a wedding!"

*A Medium Cake of
the Most Beautiful Fruits*

"And *I* forgot! There is also a medium cake of the most beautiful fruits," The Beautiful Librarian says.

"Victories against evil should *always* be celebrated in the grandest of fashions," Captain Every says.

As the magnificent desserts are brought to the center of the table, and as Button watches carefully for any luscious bits to be dropped, Henry can feel it—the adventures ahead, the catastrophes, the near misses, the great escapes. They *all* feel it; each of them does, but Henry especially. As the splendid sea stretches and crashes outside, as the great beam of the striped lighthouse circles the sky, he can practically *see* all the tales of triumph and disaster that are meant to be his.

But wait, you ask, since it is clear that you have nearly reached the end of this story. What about Mrs. Trembly, and Mr. Reese, and the terrible Mr. Needleman? What about that look that passed between Henry and Pirate Girl, and what was the meaning of that bad feeling Henry got about Apollo? Did Pirate Girl's father even notice she was gone? Will Henry live forever in that horrible house? Is there truly such a thing as Tuna Tofu?

Well, Henry has all of these questions, too, of course, right as those generous wedges of dessert are slipped onto his plate. Right as he takes that plate and remembers to say thank you and sets the beautiful dish in front of him. Right as all of his new friends look at each other with glee.

But stories are ongoing things, like the wide sea and the large sky, like goodness and evil and cruelty and love and time. And while clocks mostly go forward, ticktocking into the who-knows-what-comes-next, sometimes they go backward, and sideways, and around. The hands spin to the past, and edge to the future, and sometimes they stop altogether at ten minutes before two.

It's ten minutes before two now. It is the perfect second for time to stop, even briefly. Henry edges his fork into the cake and brings a bite to his mouth. He closes his eyes to savor the goodness. It is, without a doubt, the most delicious moment of his life.

Acknowledgments

This book wouldn't exist without Jen Klonsky and Michael Bourret, who shared my vision and brought it to life, with fun and joy and a singular like-mindedness. Oh, I love these two. Huge, huge thanks to our talented design team: Theresa Evangelista, Tony Sahara, Patrick Faricy (our incredible cover artist), and Adam Nickel (who created our delightful map). Gratitude as well to Laurel Robinson, Jacqueline Hornberger, Allyson Floridia, Caitlin Tutterow, Vanessa DeJesús, and our whole sales team. Big appreciation, too, to Carmela Iaria, Trevor Ingerson, Venessa Carson, and Summer Ogata.

Special thanks to Sonya Sones, whose friendship and wise words led directly to this book. And to my family: love, love, love. You, too, Max.

About the Author

Deb Caletti lives in a far north corner of the world. She is frightened of squirrels, owns a splendid pocketknife, and writes on an Underwood Standard Typewriter, 14 inch.

An Underwood Standard Typewriter, 14 Inch